D1015242

MARRIAGE
IS
MURDER?

A POSIE PARKER MYSTERY #9

L. B. HATHAWAY

WHITEHAVEN MAN PRESS

London

First published in Great Britain in 2020 by
Whitehaven Man Press, London

Copyright © L.B. Hathaway 2020

(http://www.lbhathaway.com, email: permissions@lbhathaway.com)

The moral right of the author, L.B. Hathaway, has been asserted.

A CIP catalogue record for this book is
available from the British Library.

ISBN (e-book:) 978-1-913531-04-1
ISBN (paperback:) 978-1-913531-05-8

For my readers

(This is not the end!)

Also by L.B. Hathaway

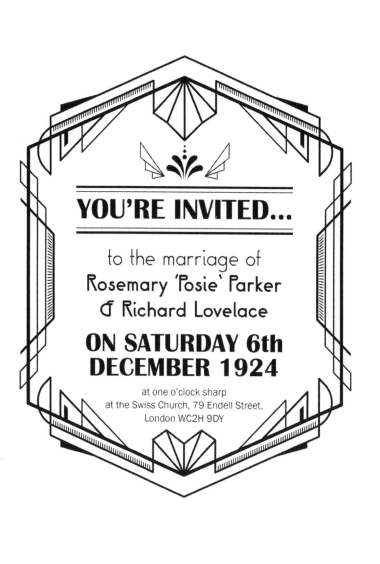

YOU'RE INVITED...

to the marriage of
Rosemary 'Posie' Parker
& Richard Lovelace

ON SATURDAY 6th
DECEMBER 1924

at one o'clock sharp
at the Swiss Church, 79 Endell Street,
London WC2H 9DY

One

Posie Parker, London's premier female Private Detective, was getting married. For real.

In her top-floor flat that morning, aided solely by Dolly, Countess of Cardigeon – her best friend – Posie had made herself ready with minimal fuss.

She'd had a long rose-scented bubble bath, read a bit of Agatha Christie's new book, *The Man in the Brown Suit*, and eaten two cheese-and-pickle sandwiches.

Then she'd stepped into her purest white silk-and-velvet wedding dress, with its matching headdress and subtle whisper of a veil. The outfit was stunning, but better still, utterly comfortable.

Like all dresses in fashion right now it was dropped-waisted and cut short at the front; just enough to see Posie's white-and-silver Mary-Jane shoes, but it pooled longer at the back, with a neat little lace-trimmed train.

Posie hadn't seen or spoken to Richard Lovelace, her fiancé, the Chief Commissioner of Scotland Yard, for a couple of days now, by prior arrangement. She hadn't even known the details of where he was spending his last night before getting married.

But Posie couldn't wait to see him, waiting for her at the altar of the Swiss Church on Endell Street; a pearl of a white church set among the tight grey criss-cross hatchwork of Bloomsbury streets, near her own flat in Museum Mansions.

The ceremony was scheduled to start at one o'clock, and Posie's ribbon-covered wedding car, a white Rolls-Royce Silver Ghost, drew up outside the church at exactly two minutes past the hour. She stepped out eagerly.

So here she was.

Finally.

Outside the church, banks of journalists and photographers, all vying for prime position on the pavement, were waiting for her in the dim December light, waving, gesturing.

'Posie Parker! You're looking a rare treat! A sight for sore eyes. He's a lucky fella, your Inspector!'

The journalists were all fairly courteous, smiling, and wishing her luck between the flash-bulbs going off. It was very cold today, and most of them were shivering in their thin trench-coats, their breath hanging icily in the air.

'This way! Turn a little, will you, Miss? Our lady readers will want to see that fancy dress. And the veil! It's for the front page of *The Times!*'

It had started to snow about an hour earlier, and a light fluffy covering lay thinly over the London pavement, coating the iron fence-rails and grey stone steps leading up to the church.

Posie looked up at the classical façade of the Swiss Church, with its graceful Doric columns on either side of the front door rising upwards to where its legend 'EGLISE SUISSE' was proudly borne. The doors were open and organ music was streaming out, striking a hopeful note. A favourite was being played, Louis Hirsch's famously jaunty 'The Wedding Glide'. Then Pachelbel's beautiful 'Canon'.

Posie was too excited to feel the cold bearing down on her.

Breathe.

Just breathe.

She readjusted her tiny skullcap and her gossamer-thin veil. One of the photographers – unusually for the profession, a woman - dashed forward, bent down and rearranged the back of Posie's dress.

'There you go, Miss. All sorted. Spectacular, if you don't mind my saying so.'

It was particularly helpful because Posie was standing here quite alone. She had no bridesmaids, no maid of honour, and no man of any sort to give her away. But that was fine: Posie had been her own woman long enough now not to mind. She took one last deep breath, and stepped into the small grey vestibule of the church.

Now.

But she knew there was something very wrong as soon as she walked in. Because the smell hit her first. It was completely wrong.

The flowers.

Posie had chosen white roses. White winter roses to be placed everywhere, heaps of the things. She'd paid for them too: the best of the best from Fortnum's. They'd cost her a small fortune.

She cursed under her breath: 'I say! What the blazes?'

The smell which overwhelmed her now was definitely not roses. A flutter of panic rose up in Posie's throat and she tried to swallow it down.

A sickly, dusky, powdery scent filled her nostrils, calling to mind holidays on the Riviera: memories of summer sun; tanning-oil on hot skin; raffia sun hats.

Mimosa.

A flower about as far removed from a December wedding in Bloomsbury as it was possible to be.

Because the dim entrance-vestibule was very small, Posie found herself literally about to step out into the main aisle. She stood very still, perched on the edge of her destiny.

People were already turning in the pews, craning their

necks, looking for their first sight of the bride. Chalky flash-lights were already going off. Candles twinkled. But Posie couldn't see individual faces among the fifty or so wedding guests; all she saw were the many bunches of yellow powdery mimosa stacked up around each pew-end, and mounted in a great pile at the front of the church on the altar there.

She had a mounting sense of growing unease. But there was no time to think any more about it, for suddenly the organ started up: Wagner's stirring 'Bridal Chorus'.

Posie slowly started to walk in time to the music with its distinctive beat. Trying to tamp down the nerves which were now fully raging, she put one Mary-Jane shoe in front of the other.

Dead slow.

The church inside was tiny, but high, everything white, rising upwards, dome-like. At the front was a small stage upon which the altar was set, the apse rising up behind, with two white-painted doors set at each side. Those wretched yellow flowers were everywhere…

I can do this.

And here was everyone she knew, at least. That was some comfort. Posie smiled nervously around.

Everyone was mish-mashed together. What seemed like crowds.

Here was Prudence, Posie's secretary, dolled up in frothy lilac, with a pale-looking Sergeant Rainbird, her own fiancé, sitting beside her with a pair of crutches and a vastly-bandaged leg, his police dress uniform with all its gold buttons shining brightly.

And here too was Len Irving, Posie's partner at the Detective Agency on Grape Street. Smart in a dark-blue winter suit. He had come with his foxy-faced sharp little snip of a wife, Aggie. And Sidney the teenage office-boy, dressed in his smartest brown-striped suit, was swallowing nervily. Next to him was his mother.

On the other side of the aisle was Richard's Housekeeper, Masha, together with little Phyllis – Richard's almost three-year-old daughter from his first marriage – in a burgundy velvet smock-coat and matching headband. They both beamed and waved at Posie as she passed, oblivious to her unease.

Further along their row Posie spotted a white-capped hospital nurse holding a very small baby. This was baby Katie. She was the newly-adopted daughter of both Posie and Richard, born back in the summer in terrible circumstances, but still too small and too sickly to come home with them; remaining, for the foreseeable future, under the care of the doctors and nurses at Great Ormond Street Hospital.

Katie had been allowed out for one hour's outing today to see her parents get married, with a special permission granted for the unusual circumstances.

There were some former clients of Posie's in attendance today: Jacinta Glaysayer, who ran a hostel for English guests out in San Gimignano, Tuscany, and a yellow-suited Felicity Fyne, a bespoke hat-maker from Hampstead.

And Evangeline Greenwood had accepted an invite, too: she was a sort of relative of Posie's, whose pre-Raphaelite-type beauty had caused many of the men in the church to simply gawp in wonder. Evangeline was certainly the most exotic and beautiful woman in the whole church, with her unfashionably-long black hair and dusky skin, her many flashing jewels and her thick Oriental velvet capes.

And here in front were several of Richard Lovelace's colleagues from work, all in their dress uniforms, all looking awfully smart.

The young but very bright Sergeant Fox and Constable Smallbone were standing together, and then next to them was an uneasy-looking Chief Inspector Oats, wearing his full police regalia, and beside him his awful wife, Matilda, sporting blood-red lipstick and a huge otter-fur coat.

Dr Poots, the Scotland Yard Pathologist, had also come. He looked much as he did in daily life, in his velvet dicky-bow-tie. Some other policemen were grouped together too, right at the front, men who looked very senior in all their glitzy epaulets and medals.

A couple of friendly journalists Posie had worked with were right at the front, all set up with their equipment, but everyone was now blurring together in tones of respectable blues, blacks, greys, maroons, browns.

Then, at the very front of the church, by contrast, in a splash of very welcome colour, was Posie's best friend, Dolly, Countess of Cardigeon, in coral-pink velvet, with deep-pink ostrich feathers all about her dainty little face, for all the world like some crazily magical petalled flower. She was together with all of her three small children and their nursemaid. Her husband, Rufus, the Earl of Cardigeon, was at her side, dressed to the nines in black tie and top hat and tails. He was Posie's dead brother's oldest friend. The only living link to a past long gone.

But through all this confusion of colours and faces and clapping hands and smiles, Posie was looking at the altar, looking for her anchor, her love. For her groom.

For Richard Lovelace – Chief Commissioner of Scotland Yard – himself.

Richard?

But he wasn't here.

Posie tried not to panic.

Looking left, she saw Richard's best man, Rhoddy Brown, his Welsh wingman from back in the days of the Great War, pacing by the altar, clutching at the ring-box. But Rhoddy, a tall and well-built man with reddish hair himself, smart in a hired set of black tie and top hat, didn't meet Posie's eye, and couldn't seem to stand still, looking backwards and forwards nervously.

Posie looked towards the Vicar.

At least *he* was here, smiling around, holding the silver-pressed Order of Service in his hands together with a prayer-book.

But hang about!

This wasn't the same man Posie and Richard Lovelace had met one week previously to discuss their rather last-minute nuptials. Father René Hoffman, a French-speaking Swiss, had been tall and thin and rather old-looking, in his late fifties at least. He had been welcoming and charming and only too willing to allow their wedding ceremony to take place in the Swiss Church, despite the fact that neither Posie nor Richard had had anything to do with it before.

This Vicar was rather the opposite of Father Hoffman: short, fat, young-ish, bespectacled, with sad-looking creased eyes with strange heavy lids, a fine head of luxurious curly brown hair. As he moved it seemed as if he had a sort of limp, or perhaps he was flat-footed: there was definitely a problem with his feet, somehow.

Posie was right at the altar now. Claustrophobically close.

She seemed to be right up against the Vicar's black cassock; the gold embroidery of the tiny crosses in their repeat pattern on his stole blurring before her eyes. The man's thick sausage-like fingers were brushing over something in his pocket. When he pulled at the pocket a black-wood rosary was exposed. A rosary? A *Catholic* rosary? Here in the protestant Swiss Church? All of these details were noticed by Posie in her rising panic.

She turned, searching for the nearest, dearest person to her. It was Dolly, whose face was a small, pale, scared-looking sun among all the pink feathers.

'Where's Richard?' Posie hissed urgently. She thought suddenly that she might cry. A huge wave of tears welled up, threatening to spill over, threatening to ruin her porcelain-powdered face, the carefully-applied Maybelline eye-black.

Posie gasped. 'Don't tell me he's…?'

'Jilted you, you mean?' Dolly's wide, pink-lipsticked smile seemed impossibly tight now, stretched to snapping-point.

'I haven't seen him, lovey. Actually, I don't think anyone has.'

****

Two

Posie's fingers were rubbing in panic against the stems of the white rose bouquet she was carrying, and she seemed to have found the only thorn, for in a second she'd ruptured her thumb. A single prick of blood fell to the floor, but the sudden pain seemed to focus her attention and made her snap into action. She handed her bouquet to Dolly, and marched over to Rhoddy Brown.

'Do you know where Richard is, Mr Brown?' she asked, trying to sound cool and calm and collected. She noticed he was wearing yellow mimosa in his buttonhole. The bright yellow clashed with his auburn hair.

'You came with him today, didn't you?'

The man in top hat and tails looked at her now, shook his head and bit at a trembling lip. 'I haven't seen Richie all morning. We were together – with some police chaps – last night in Soho. We took in some dancing at a club. Had dinner at Kettner's, but we all parted at the Underground, Miss. At Leicester Square. Around eleven o'clock. Richie took the Northern line to Clapham to go home to his kiddie. I walked back to the boarding-house he'd kindly organised for me, just around the corner here in Bloomsbury. I presume he arrived home?'

Posie called over to Masha. 'Did Richard come home last night? Have you seen him at all this morning?'

But Masha was shaking her head, panic showing in her blue, Slavic-tilted eyes. 'He no come home, Madam. I no understand. Why would he come back to Clapham, Miss Parker? Make no sense. All his things already at your place. All *our* things too! We all move into your apartment tomorrow, no? Nothing left in Clapham. House all sold up and new people arrive tomorrow to live there. So last night I think he is with you! I think you are staying together, no?'

'The night before a *wedding*?' brayed the very English-sounding Vicar in snooty tones of utter disbelief. And everybody turned to him.

'Who the blazes are *you*?' snapped Posie, angry now. 'Where is Father Hoffman?'

'He's sick, I'm afraid. I thought he had managed to telephone to you both yesterday? No? Oh dear. Well, it can't be helped. Terrible winter flu still going the rounds, I hear. I'm the locum priest for this area: Camden and Bloomsbury. I'm the Reverend Jimmy Gibbons. I can do both sides of the coin, Protestant and Catholic, if needed. Handy, eh? Although I gather there's not much of anything required today.'

He made a show of looking at some scribbled notes on the back of his Order of Service.

'Yes: the notes I got given say "*BE AS BRIEF AS POSSIBLE, INCLUDE A BIT OF PRAYER AND A SNATCH OF ANGLICAN-STYLE CEREMONY FOR THE BRIDE – HER FATHER WAS AN ANGLICAN VICAR – BUT DON'T GO OVERBOARD. THE GROOM DOESN'T REALLY MIND AS LONG AS HE GETS HIS GIRL.*" So, is there a problem, Miss Parker?'

The Reverend Gibbons adjusted his round gold spectacles, and peered at Posie in a kindly fashion from his sad, creased eyes. It seemed he was very short-sighted.

'Yes, there is a problem,' said Posie matter-of-factly, but underneath it all her heart was beating wildly. 'My groom has not turned up. He is not here to get his girl at all.'

Oh, Richard, where are you? Posie thought to herself with mounting horror.

Everything had seemed fine between them just a couple of days ago, and Richard had obviously enjoyed a sort of celebration the evening before, as he had told her he would, with Rhoddy Brown.

Although it sounded bigger and wilder than he had mentioned it would be. He certainly hadn't said anything about any dancing clubs in Soho. But well: why not?

Posie's blood froze.

Had Richard got cold feet? Had he questioned her loyalty, or her love, to him?

Was Richard Lovelace walking away somewhere right now, or speeding somewhere on a train, running from this wedding ceremony they had planned together? Running away from the future he and Posie had imagined would be intertwined together, forever?

Posie turned and caught the eyes of little Phyllis, her soon-to-be stepdaughter. An excitement and happiness burned in Phyllis' brown, trusting eyes. Posie loved Phyllis almost as much as she loved Lovelace himself.

No.

Sure as bread was bread, Richard Lovelace would not have walked out on this ceremony with Posie, and certainly would not have left his little daughter to witness the resulting mess. All of this was completely uncharacteristic.

Posie turned to the congregation. She cleared her throat and addressed everybody:

'Is anybody able to tell me if they have seen Richard – my fiancé – at all, today?'

She looked about wildly, catching and meeting the eyes of dozens of people. All she registered there were negative shakes of the head, confusion and a mounting sadness apparent in almost everybody's gaze.

A dumb embarrassment at what looked like Posie's ultimate misfortune and shame was beginning to sink

in, weigh down on everybody. The same thought – s*he's
been jilted. Jilted! How dreadful!* – obviously coming to the
forefront of every mind.

This was not how it was supposed to be.

So far in Posie's thirty-two years of life she had lost a
great deal.

Her mother had walked out on the family when Posie
was still very young, and her brother, also called Richard,
had died in 1917 in Messines, doing battle in the Great
War. Her father, a Vicar, had died of a broken heart just a
couple of years later, leaving Posie quite alone.

And through a variety of circumstances, Posie had
managed to lose two previous fiancés before having become
engaged to Richard Lovelace. Quite a track record, in fact.

It seemed she had now lost a third.

Was she destined to remain unmarried? Part of those vast
hordes of single women of her own age who would remain
spinsters forever, following the losses of the Great War
which had wiped out most of the men of her generation?

*I will not cry. I will not. Richard has not left me. He wanted
this as much as me.*

More, actually.

Posie closed her eyes for a moment, struggling for
clarity, certainty, a way forward. *Somehow, I must find him.*

She breathed in the thick, powdery air of the mimosa,
that cloying scent which was mixing unattractively with
the bleach and almost industrial-smelling cleanliness of
the Swiss Church.

Here, there was no reassuring church perfume of musty
hymn-books and old lead roofing, mixed in with moulding
vestments. This place was not like Posie's father's old church
back in Norfolk, where she had grown up. It was not like
the thousands of medieval little Anglican churches which
dotted the country, with that same special scent pervading
all of them: the scent of centuries of worship, and decay,
and trust, and loss.

Even the banks of burning candles here seemed to be odourless. This church had been chosen by her and Richard for what it represented: cleanliness; neutrality; a welcoming and bright new start.

Posie opened her eyes, facing down the wall of pity which met her.

She turned to the locum priest. 'This is not your fault,' she said, 'and I thank you for stepping into the breach, Reverend Gibbons. My apologies if I was rude to you just now.'

She turned back to the congregation. 'Please bear with me. A good deal of things seem odd to me here. Golly, it's as if I am attending quite the wrong wedding! Not my own. First, does anybody have any idea who sent this mimosa, or where all my white roses have gone? I saw the roses being unloaded on Endell Street myself, last night. I watched the men from Fortnum's bring them inside the church! Call me a perfectionist, but I wanted to make sure things were going to be fine. Anybody?'

There was a silence, and a lot of shaking of heads, sympathy flooding the place.

Posie looked over again at Rhoddy Brown, the best man. In fact, this was the first time she had ever met Brown, who lived in the hard-to-reach valleys of Wales, although Posie had spoken to him on the telephone once or twice in the past few months and had read his letters to Richard, which were usually very funny and full of a dry sense of humour.

Rhoddy's wife was a chronic asthmatic and she was bed-bound, and he barely left her. Richard was always full of praise for Rhoddy Brown, a gunner who had shown loyalty and determination in the trenches, saving Richard's life twice. And it was this same loyalty and determination Rhoddy now showed towards his ill wife on a daily basis, which endeared him to Richard still. It was quite something he had managed to travel up to London to be

Richard's best man, especially with only one week's notice. An honour. Posie vowed she would be calm and civil to the man if it was the last thing she did.

'Rhoddy, you said you went to Kettner's? Do you think it's possible Richard returned there? Was anybody else here at the dinner, please?'

Rhoddy looked about him nervously, then shook his head. 'There were about twelve of us, Miss Parker. All police lads, the others were. Wearin' uniforms, very smart and tidy. I'm sure of it, so I am. But I can't see anyone here now who was with us.'

Posie frowned. 'Was anyone else here at Richard's dinner last night? There were ten other policemen? Who were they? Anyone?'

There were men here in the congregation whom Richard surely would have invited to a big special dinner, wouldn't he? Rufus, for example. All of the policeman Posie knew, definitely.

But no.

Everybody here on the Scotland Yard team were shaking their heads. Most, especially Chief Inspector Oats, were looking uncomfortable and disappointed. Embarrassed at the lack of an invite.

This didn't seem right at all. Most strange.

'Rainbird, *you* weren't there?'

Rainbird, looking slightly upset, indicated towards his broken leg and waved a crutch. 'How could I have been, Miss? I was in hospital until this morning. I got a special discharge just to attend your wedding.'

'Of course. I'm so sorry. I'm a little nervous here.'

How thoughtless of her! Poor Rainbird had been working on a case with both Posie and Lovelace six weeks previously on the coast and had ended up pretty badly injured. In fact, he was downright lucky to be alive.

Posie's eyes met Sergeant Fox's grey-green gaze, and his lean, fair, wolfhound-like face with its strange hungry beauty gave her comfort just now, right at this dreadful moment.

'I need you, Sergeant. I need you to help me. Get over to Kettner's right now. See if *they* can tell you anything about Richard, last night, or this morning. Anything at all. Maybe he was taken ill and went back there. Or he left something behind? Check Leicester Square Underground Station too: maybe they know something, saw something? And check at our hotel, where we have the Wedding Breakfast set up for you all. 'The Montague on the Gardens' next to the British Museum. Maybe Richard went there last night? I do know it's clutching at straws, but…'

Fox nodded diligently, but didn't look hopeful. 'I'll go right away, Miss. Of course. You can trust me.'

But as he ran down the aisle and left the church, a strange tapping noise began. It was a peculiar sound, both near and yet far-off: echoing all around.

Everybody started to look about.

TAP. TAP-TAP. TAP.

'What's that horrid funny noise?' called out Phyllis Lovelace, fear in her little voice.

The Reverend Gibbons was looking all about him anxiously.

'I don't know this church, not at all. Mnnn, there doesn't even seem to be a proper vestry here. What's that door over there?' He pointed at the white door nearest him, on the right-hand side of the apse. 'Is the noise coming from in there?'

Just then a small bent-over little man appeared, in his fifties maybe, but in poor health obviously, shuffling up the aisle. He was holding onto a sheaf of papers, and he indicated behind him, upwards.

Posie frowned, taking in the magnificent organ set in a white balcony above the front door which she hadn't registered on arrival, being too preoccupied with herself and her own situation. She didn't understand who this man was or what he meant with all his wild gesticulations.

'Sorry? Who are you, sir?'

The man put out a hand. 'The Organist of the Swiss Church. Mr Berryman, at your service, Miss.'

'Oh! Er, delighted. We're looking for the source of this noise…'

The tapping was growing louder, more urgent.

'That's why I came down, Miss. I know this place well. I must be the only one here today who does, eh?' He pointed towards the door the Vicar was showing an interest in. 'That door there is only a fire escape. Literally a windowless corridor which takes one on a merry little walk to an outside covered alleyway, which comes around to the front of the next-door building, leading one onto Endell Street again. I don't think this wretched tapping is coming from there, Miss. But would you like to come with me and see?'

But before she could answer, Constable Smallbone had jumped forward, slipping his uniformed arm through the little man's arm, moving forward towards the right-hand door.

'*I'll* do this, Miss. Check out this fire escape. You stay there, Miss. Back in two minutes.'

'Thank you.'

Posie was looking all about her, with everybody else. The noise was insistent now. Echoing about the place, so amplified that you couldn't exactly say *where* its source was.

'Old pipes?' suggested the Reverend Gibbons, shrugging slightly. 'These churches are all the same in winter.'

'Not this one,' said Posie stubbornly. 'This place is well looked-after. It's not the same at all.'

And then Smallbone and the Organist reappeared. Smallbone shook his head in disappointment:

'Nah, nothing doing, Miss. It's exactly as this chappie described: a brick alleyway with nothing in it except loads of dirty-looking tulip boxes stinking of earth. Good job you didn't come: you would have muddied your nice white dress. Rest assured, no-one's down there and no-one's been down there, Miss. There was no noise at all. We couldn't hear anything. Only when we got back in here.'

Just then the banging and tapping got even louder.
TAP. TAP-TAP. TAP.

And then there was a muffled shout.

* * * *

Three

Rhoddy Brown bounded over to the identical white door on the left-hand side of the apse. He shouted out excitedly: 'It's coming from in *here*!'

He wrenched it open, flinging the door back smartly. But then he stood back, disappointed, running his hands through his thick red hair.

'But how can it be? There's nothing in here, Miss Parker. It's only a service cupboard, so it is. Stuffed full of bric-a-brac! Anyone else want to come and have a look? Although the banging *does* seem to be coming from this area of the room…'

TAP. TAP-TAP. TAP.

The three Cardigeon children – the small twins Trixie and Bunny, and their little baby brother Raymond – had started jumping up and down on the pew next to their parents, and screaming. There seemed precious little their nursemaid could do about it. Phyllis Lovelace was looking at the Cardigeon children, wide-eyed and jealous and fearful, all in equal measure. She tested out a few bleats of her own. It added to the general chaos.

The tapping got more insistent although there were no more shouts. And into this almighty chaos stepped an unlikely hero.

'Now, then. You little nippers can just pipe down, and everybody else please stay where they are.'

Chief Inspector Oats, resplendent in his navy-and-gold regalia was up on his feet now and seemed to have taken some sort of control. Even the Cardigeon children shut up.

Oats walked to the very back of the church, to the tiny vestibule.

'First off, I am going to go and deal with those blimmin' journalists waiting outside,' he said firmly. 'Next, I want you, Smallbone, to go around the inside of this little church, step by bleedin' step if necessary, listening to the walls, and locate what this dreadful ruckus is. There was definitely a human shout just then. We'll get to the bottom of this; you'll see if we don't, Miss Parker. Or I'll eat my hat.'

Posie stared at the Inspector's retreating back, feeling thankful to him for perhaps the first time in her life. She felt like crying as the tapping continued, and then over it all, a telephone started ringing.

Posie stood as if frozen, right in front of the altar, at the head of the aisle. What on earth? *Was this Richard? Could it be?*

'Where can that telephone apparatus be located?' the small priest was saying at her side, looking about in some anguish. 'I say, this is really a most irregular set of affairs!'

Oats reappeared from outside, excitement showing in his fishy blue eyes. 'It's here! The bleedin' telephone equipment is here in this hallway!'

The shrill ringing of the telephone stopped abruptly as Oats grabbed at the telephone receiver in the vestibule. Everybody in the Swiss Church swivelled around and listened to him, above the din of the tapping.

'Scotland Yard, you say? Calling here? Well, most of us are *here*! This is a mare's nest, no doubt about it. Yes, put them through. I'll hold the line. Chief Inspector Bill Oats speaking.'

In the seconds of waiting that elapsed, Smallbone had completed an entire lap of the interior of the Swiss

Church, ending up on the stage at the very front, next to the left-hand doorway.

'It's here! Yes: it's definitely around here!' shouted Smallbone as he joined Rhoddy Brown.

Posie bounded up onto the stage herself, holding up her veil and her train with its shimmering, silver-threaded snippets of glimmer running through it.

She joined the men at the left-hand door, but Brown was right. It was simply a shallow cupboard, perhaps only one-foot deep inside. The white shelves were filled with innumerable objects all relating to church services. Hundreds of objects. Candles, hymn-books, old vases. Even an old box of confetti which must surely have been pressed before the Great War?

TAP. TAP.

'Hang about!' said Smallbone excitedly, putting his whole head inside the cupboard, pressing his ear against the back of a shelf. 'The noise is definitely coming from *inside* here.' He turned to the congregation. 'Be quiet, everyone! I need a moment of absolute quiet.'

Silence came over the church. And in that silence a man's voice could just about be heard.

'Help! Help me, please!'

The voice was frail and tinny, sounding as if it was coming from far away. The banging started up again.

'Where are you?' shouted Posie, exasperated and fearful.

It had not been a voice she recognised, but who knew?

She pressed her fingers, the nails all painted in pale-pink shellac nail varnish, up against the cool, white-and-grey marble walls around the cupboard, then along the walls which formed the apse. The marble had a deadening effect, she was sure. Perhaps it distorted voices? Surely the man couldn't be stuck behind *here*? That would be like being walled up alive in a tomb, wouldn't it?

How dreadful. It didn't bear thinking about.

It couldn't be Richard. It couldn't.

She'd have known his voice anywhere, even behind a wall of marble. But it didn't stop the rising tide of fear within her. She turned to the two men, and the Vicar who had hurried over.

'He's definitely in here. *Someone's* in here,' she said, seriously. 'But how can we get in?'

But everybody had turned again, for Inspector Oats had walked into the main church, seeming to take up all the space in the narrow aisle. His face showed real confusion.

'Miss Parker, that was the Yard calling. Sorry that took a moment. Most unusual. Apparently, they took receipt of a thousand white roses about an hour-and-a-half ago.'

A dreadful gasp came up from the congregation, with everybody turning, as one, to look at Posie.

'My wedding flowers!'

'Well, that's as maybe, Miss,' said Oats, shrugging. 'The flowers have only just been looked at and registered in the books, I'm afraid, what with it being a Saturday and all. The Duty Sergeant gathered them together as best he could, stuffed them in our Lost Property cupboard, and while he was doing that, he saw there was a note placed in among them, addressed to you, Miss. It even gave the exchange and church telephone number for the Sergeant to call. Very handy. He called through to here as soon as he read it.'

Posie stepped to the edge of the stage, fearful. 'What did the note say?'

'Well, it seems like some kind of riddle, or a joke or something, Miss. It's quite long. Are you ready?'

'Of course I am.' Posie now sat down on the edge of the stage. She was trying not to tremble. Dolly came to sit beside her friend and held her hand.

In her nervousness, Dolly started to flick open and shut her tiny ruby-encrusted Houbigant powder compact.

Open and shut. Open and shut.

The disc of pressed powder inside came unglued and

fell out, landing in bright orange clumps all over Dolly' lap, and over Posie's dress and shoes. But Posie was now past caring.

'I will quote it exactly,' Oats began, looking down at his ever-present police notepad:

"*There will be no wedding.*

But have no fear, Lovelace is near.

Locked in tight, there'll be no respite.

A river runs by, and time rings high.

A cosy little room for a missing groom!

You won't become his wife, but this will still be the happiest day of your life."

Oats coughed uncomfortably. 'I can't make head nor tail of this myself, Miss. Except that it seems…'

'…Someone has kidnapped Richard,' said Posie, matter-of-factly.

* * * *

Four

Baby Katie had started to cry, wild and high-shrieking screams in her tiny, cat-like mewling voice. The tapping continued, but there was no more shouting.

In all the din, Posie tried to focus on details.

She was aware of Dolly still at her side, patting at her hand. 'It will be fine, lovey, you'll see it will.'

But Dolly sounded less than reassuring and Posie watched as her friend abandoned the powder compact and instead dug out a pink-and-black Sobranie cocktail cigarette from a silver case she'd tucked within the folds of her pink velvet dress, and lit it expertly, taking a deep drag. Dolly was then doubled-up coughing, hacking over and over.

You won't become his wife…

Posie ran over those awful lines again. She stared up into nothingness, on past the organ in its balcony, on past the white walls. She wanted to scream aloud: *Oh, Richard, how did this happen?*

But then another terrible question entered her mind: *was Richard dead?*

That awful little note had spoken of Richard being locked in, but hadn't actually said anything about whether Richard was still alive, had it?

Posie pushed the thought to the back of her mind, because that way madness lay; she should focus on assuming Richard was still alive, albeit indisposed.

It seemed that somehow they had managed – between the two of them – to encounter some crazy madman who had taken it upon himself to sabotage their wedding in order to cause maximum chaos and disruption, and to cause hurt to both parties.

But who could that be?

Richard Lovelace's enemies were legion, that much was true.

He'd foiled hundreds of gangs across London, splicing open various plans for murders and robberies before they had even happened. He'd managed over several years to put behind bars several of the capital's most hardened, dangerous criminals. Maybe these criminals had relatives or employees or agents who had plotted to put Richard Lovelace out of action on what should have been the happiest day of his life?

There was a bottomless, fathomless pit of people to choose from: it was too difficult to try and pounce on a single name right here, right now, with no evidence to speak of.

And as for Posie herself, and enemies. Well, there *had* been one. But he was most probably long dead…

'Gracious me! What *is* that bally noise? It's not stopping, is it?'

Rufus, the Eleventh Earl of Cardigeon, was now up on the stage too, sweaty and red-looking in his black tie and tails, the whole outfit slightly too small for him: he had put on a lot of weight recently.

Rufus raced to the white cupboard door, huffing and puffing as he went, and suddenly, as if he had quite lost his mind, he started pulling items out from the white shelves within. 'Help me, won't you, man?' he instructed Smallbone, who started to follow suit.

In moments like this, Posie found it easier to find some kind of quiet within the storm. She slipped off the stage-edge, and went down to where Oats was still standing, as if frozen. She took his notepad from him silently and for once he put up no protest. She read again the note he had transcribed from the Duty Sergeant at Scotland Yard.

But have no fear, Lovelace is near.

Could Richard be *here*? Was that actually him – somehow far off – they could hear behind the marble wall?

Suddenly, Sergeant Fox came bounding into the church. He marched up to the stage-area.

'The Chief's not at Kettner's, Miss,' he reported excitedly. 'But there's something strange about all that, Miss,' he said quickly. 'In fact, more than strange.'

He looked across at Rhoddy Brown, who was now aiding Rufus and Smallbone, taking out all of the contents of the shelves, making a heap on the floor. For such a big man he moved quickly, fluidly. Chief Inspector Oats had gone up to join them now. Fox called out to the Welshman:

'Mr Brown, sir, are you sure you were at *Kettner's* last night? Not some other place? Because the Restaurant Manager said he has no recollection of a stag party eating on their premises last night. No large group of men at all.'

The Welshman wiped sweat from his brow and shook his head at Fox in disbelief.

''Course, sir. I even went as far as to take a couple of twists of their matches with me to take home to my wife, sir. It will be a rare treat for her to see them.' He patted his breast pocket. 'And I was that excited to be in the West End of London, I'd not forget the name of the place. Maybe we didn't seem like a stag party? We weren't rowdy at all: not like some others might have behaved.'

Fox frowned, but then shrugged. 'Odd. I asked at Leicester Square Underground Station, too, but they hadn't seen a thing. But I had more luck at the hotel, at The Montague, Miss.'

'Oh?' Posie's interest, strung tight, almost snapped in her eagerness.

'He stayed there last night, Miss. I suppose in your, *ahem…*' the Sergeant coloured up red, then checked himself and carried on, '…in your Wedding Suite, Miss. He ordered breakfast to his room this morning, at nine o'clock: kippers and the full English. He'd asked for his dress shirt to be ironed overnight and it was sent up this morning by a maid, and he gave her a tip. He was *seen*, Miss, by at least two of the hotel staff. I checked the descriptions. Definitely him.' Fox's eyes flashed triumphantly, encouragingly:

'So, he was safe at nine o'clock this morning. And the Chief was definitely preparing to get married to you, Miss!'

'Thank you, Sergeant Fox. That *is* good news.'

He hasn't left you.

'There's more, Miss. He was also seen this morning a bit later on, about eleven-ish, by the fella on reception. The Chief was on his way out, in a tearing hurry. It's possible he had a man with him, but the reception fella couldn't swear on it. The Chief was dressed in his police dress uniform and cap already, and he told the reception fella he had some urgent business to attend to. He'd received a worrying telephone call up in his room.'

'Business? Telephone call? A man? I wonder what Richard was up to…'

Posie looked down at the note again, still trying to extract some kind of meaning from it, staring at Oats' clear, round handwriting as if it might be the Holy Grail itself.

Locked in tight, there'll be no respite. A river runs by, and time rings high.

What did that mean? It sounded so familiar.

And then the Vicar was with her again. The Reverend Jimmy Gibbons looking earnest and concerned. He tapped at his gold wristwatch a little regretfully.

'I'm afraid, Miss Parker, that, under normal circumstances, this wedding ceremony would be drawing to a close just now. As a locum priest, I am, I'm afraid, in great demand all over this part of London today. In fact, I'm supposed to be presiding over another wedding ceremony at St George's Church on Bloomsbury Way in less than twenty minutes' time. It's only a short distance, but what with the snow it may take me a little longer than usual to walk there… I do hope you won't find it rude if I make my excuses and leave? Of course, this is a highly regretful and sad situation. In my whole time in Holy Orders I have only presided over a "jilted at the altar" situation once before. And I had hoped never to repeat it.'

Jilted at the altar?

Posie looked across into the man's podgy, doughy, unremarkable face and felt like slapping it. But that would be the height of bad manners. And it wasn't his fault, either, was it?

She nodded, tightly. 'Of course you should go, Reverend. I quite understand. In fact, I am about to tell the rest of the congregation to go on to The Montague Hotel where there is a full Wedding Breakfast laid out for them. Better not let that food go to waste. Not like my lovely flowers… Besides, the children will be hungry now, and fractious.'

Flowers.

Posie looked all about her at the yellow mimosa.

She bit her lip and looked across at Len Irving, her business partner. She had once fancied herself in love with him, thought him indispensable to her happiness, in what seemed like a lifetime ago.

Back then, personal circumstances had sent Len off suddenly and without warning to the South of France, and Posie had received a bouquet of mimosa from France around the same time, and, missing Len dreadfully, it had made her day. She had believed wholeheartedly it was from Len; the epitome of romance, the height of romantic gestures.

But the sender of the mimosa way back then had not, in

fact, been Len; it had been her arch enemy. Her *one* enemy. Count Caspian della Rosa.

A man she had seen shot, probably fatally, before he had disappeared off the face of the earth more than a year and a half ago.

Len Irving caught her eye.

So far in all of this ruckus he had been sitting beside his wife, Aggie, with the look of someone who waits, rather than acts. Now he sprung up.

'Show us that, Posie, love,' he said quickly, joining her. He ran his hands through his dark curling hair, now slightly tinged with grey at the temples, and his quick sparkling eyes were alert with tension. Len took the notepad from Posie's hands and read the message out loud.

A river runs by, and time rings high.

'Oh!' Posie said quickly and certainly. 'I've got it, Len!'

'Me too: great minds think alike, eh?'

They looked at each other, these two who had shared so much and yet so little. They both grinned, before saying together: 'SCOTLAND YARD!'

How could Posie have been so slow?

Lovelace wasn't here at all, was he? He wasn't trapped behind a marble wall. He wasn't at Kettner's. He'd stayed at 'their' hotel before being summoned into work for some 'urgent business' which had cropped up. Most likely the urgent business had been a ruse. It had probably been a fake summons; false pretences.

Richard Lovelace had gone to his office.

A beautiful office which he had acquired only a month or so earlier, when he'd taken on the prestigious role of Chief Commissioner. It was an office set high in the building of New Scotland Yard, right next to the Embankment. Richard's office looked out over the River Thames – *a river runs by* – with one window looking directly out over the Houses of Parliament, and Big Ben – *time rings high* – with its famous clock tower.

Yes: she was certain of it, and Posie now addressed the church accordingly.

'I think Richard is at his Scotland Yard office! He's been locked in. I need to go there now. Quick as can be. Get him out.'

Posie was galvanised into action. 'Prudence, can you get all the guests together and walk them over to The Montague Hotel and start eating? Act as if nothing untoward has happened. Eat the wedding cake if needs be. It's only five minutes from here but it may take longer in all of this snow.' She nodded at Rainbird with his crutches. 'And for goodness' sake, *you* go carefully.'

She turned to where Rufus was now hurling himself at the inside of the now-empty cupboard on the left-hand side of the apse. Rhoddy Brown was kicking and heaving at the wood as well, as if his life depended on it, sweat running down his red, puffy face. Chief Inspector Oats was standing well back, with the young policemen, all of them muttering together and exchanging meaning-laden looks.

Posie called out to them:

'Sergeant Fox and Constable Smallbone, please stay here and try and sort out whatever is going on beyond that marble wall. Call in reinforcements if necessary.'

The policemen nodded, slightly sheepish at their own inaction.

She looked at the Welshman, hot, panting, taking a moment to get his breath back. 'Mr Brown, thank you for your help. I'm sorry about this strange set of circumstances that we are finally meeting in. I hope to chat to you more later, *with* Richard.'

'Of course, Miss. That sounds lovely.'

Dolly had jumped off the stage, and was grabbing at something from under her pew, her beautiful velvet gown pooling behind her on the floor. She stood up, and to Posie's complete astonishment she was holding up Posie's very own beloved carpet bag. It looked very worn and a trifle grubby in here. Dolly tucked it under her arm.

'I'm coming with you, Posie. I had a feeling, for some reason, that you might be needing this today.' She waved the bulky bag at Posie. Posie saw the row of small, keen faces in the pew behind, at all the little Cardigeons looking up at her anxiously. Posie shook her head.

'No, Dolly. You stay with your children.'

Dolly was a mother, and these little children needed her. Posie could not be held accountable for dragging Dolly into whatever danger she herself was about to step into.

Posie watched Rufus jumping about, literally smashing his shoulder into wood which cracked beneath his weight. No: he wouldn't do either. He should stay here too.

Posie was aware that everybody was watching her. She checked her wristwatch. It was one forty-five.

She nodded at the congregation: 'I'm going alone. The wedding car will still be waiting outside, I hope. I'll take that across town. It won't take long, even with all this snow. It's Saturday, so the roads won't be busy between here and Scotland Yard: no commuters, no businesspeople thronging the streets. I will get there and back in a jiffy, you'll see.'

Taking her carpet bag, which seemed heavier than usual, Posie marched towards the exit.

Chief Inspector Oats followed her.

'I'm going to telephone to the Yard now, Miss,' he said quickly, assuredly. 'I'll give them an early warning, ask them to get up to the Chief Commissioner's office, check everything is fine. But I'll get in the next motor-taxi which comes along and be there myself shortly. Right behind you.'

'Thank you. I'm grateful.'

And she meant it.

Posie had a brief glimpse of blurred faces about her as she left. She caught sight of the efficient-looking nurse from Great Ormond Street Hospital, holding the tiny bundle that was baby Katie, who should so shortly be coming to join them as a family.

What kind of impression would this nurse be taking back to the hospital from all of this? Posie thought to herself grimly.

That a couple of professional, fairly high-ranking people could not even make a go of getting married to each other was surely some sort of sick joke? A complete mess. Posie hoped beyond hope that baby Katie would still be allowed to come to them when all of this was over.

Darting through the small porch, Posie heard Oats placing a call to the Operator on the church telephone equipment, and she then became aware of a swaying figure in black-and-white vestments moving ahead of her, as the Reverend Jimmy Gibbons went tap-tapping flat-footedly along the snowy pavement in the direction of Bloomsbury and the British Museum, on his way to his next wedding ceremony at St George's Church.

He had donned a black biretta-style hat and was carrying a useful-looking black-and-gold cane with which to add stability on the slippery streets.

Mercifully, the white Rolls-Royce Silver Ghost was still outside, as was a small gaggle of journalists, even though Oats had obviously done his best at getting rid of most of them.

Posie flung open the car door, and clambered in, grabbing up her veil and small train behind her.

She was aware of the journalists staring at her, open-mouthed, goggling.

Where was the groom? Where was the Chief Commissioner in all of this?

Why was the famous Posie Parker, on her wedding day, getting into the wedding car, leaving the church at which she was supposed to be getting married, all alone?

Posie sat back on the green leather seat and wondered the same thing herself.

'Go! Go! Go!' she almost screamed at the driver; whose surprised gaze met her anxious eyes in the front mirror.

'Right you are then, Miss.'

* * * *

Five

But as Posie sped away, with Chief Inspector Oats stepping down onto the icy pavement to hail a passing motor-taxi just behind her, she could hardly have been aware of what was unfolding in the church she had left behind.

It was exactly the sort of danger she wouldn't have wished upon her worst enemy, let alone those nearest and dearest to her.

A nightmare, in fact.

Because, the moment Chief Inspector Oats left the building, Rufus Cardigeon – with brute force – had managed to rip down the white shelves inside the cupboard, and the smashed and splintered wood fell forward into his hands, fresh screws still intact, the whole thing insubstantial as a stage-set.

'What the deuce?' he had puffed, turning to the policemen around him. 'I say! This is a bally fake cupboard. There's a small room behind here!'

And then he and the two young policemen were stepping inside the black cavernous space – about as big as an average larder – which was revealed within, and Sergeant Fox shouted out for all the congregation, now standing, to hear:

'There's someone in here! A fella! We've got him! It's all fine!'

And between them Fox and Smallbone had carried a gagged and bound man out from the space. Bending down, they had tugged off the man's gag hurriedly, putting him into a sitting-upright position to try and cut the ropes off his hands and ankles as painlessly as possible. Everybody in the congregation was staring hard at the man on the stage, and nudging each other.

Who was he? Did anybody recognise this man?

The man was dark-haired and sickly-yellow in the face, very slight and fragile-looking, in his early forties, unremarkable-looking, dressed smartly in a blue pinstriped suit which had obviously seen better days. The man didn't look well at all. He was shivering uncontrollably and the two policemen had flung off their own thick navy dress jackets, wrapping him around with them, rubbing at his wrists and ankles to bring back circulation.

'He's freezing cold! He's got the shakes! Anyone got brandy or whisky on them?' shouted out Sergeant Fox to the stunned congregation.

Len Irving had hurried forward with a hip-flask of brandy and was helping the man drink a little.

But then the focus shifted and everyone stared in complete disbelief as a jacket-less Rufus – sweaty and dusty and white-paint flecked – emerged at the open door of the cupboard, and in his arms he was carrying someone else. A slight, fragile-looking old man, wearing Rufus' black jacket over his own black garments, was bound in a similar way to the first man, but with no gag.

'There's a corridor leading off that room, lads,' said Rufus breathlessly. 'Good job *I* went off down it to investigate and found this fella. Not like you two police boys! Shame on you, I say! So excited you couldn't look just a little further on! *This* was the gentleman we heard shouting out and tapping, bless him,' said Rufus, scowling down at the policemen.

He laid the old man on the stage gently next to the first

man and Len offered the same brandy while the Sergeants worked to cut the old man's ties.

'He'd obviously got his gag off and has almost lost his bally voice through shouting out,' said Rufus. 'It's a miracle we could hear him actually, the wall is dashed thick. He keeps saying something about the organ. *This* organ?' He pointed over to the beautiful organ mounted in its balcony on the wall, then bent lower again to the man he had just rescued.

'What do you mean, old fellow?'

But the second the old man on the floor opened his mouth to speak, there was a sudden volley of gunshots, all fired into the high apse of the Swiss Church, and everybody dived for cover under their pews.

The echoing sound, like fireworks going off, had everybody screaming, the children in particular, and in the awful sudden silence which followed, the policemen on the stage by the altar, together with Rufus, were just able to see a flurry of action over by the main door as several men from the congregation left the church in a stampede.

A loud bang and a key turning in a lock indicated that the door to the Swiss Church was now firmly shut and bolted.

Sergeant Fox was on his feet and shouting out now:

'Is everybody all right? Is anyone hurt? I think whoever was shooting has gone.'

And in all the chaos as people emerged from under the pews and chairs, another sound of tapping and moaning had begun.

But this time it came from up within the balcony where the organ was housed.

* * * *

Six

As Posie had predicted, the roads to Scotland Yard were virtually empty.

The cold wintry weather and the pelting snow had ensured that most Londoners were staying very firmly and snugly inside on this Saturday afternoon.

As the beautiful Silver Ghost hurtled down the Kingsway, Posie noticed how there was not a soul in sight walking under the plane-tree-lined avenue. Shops and cafés were closing early and small shivering boys with sandwich-boards were queueing outside the Lyons Cornerhouse on the Strand, desperate to hand the boards back and get their tuppence worth of pay.

The silence was eerie.

All along the Strand, on past Charing Cross, the blur of white was coming down faster, turning pavements and familiar landmarks into an unknown winter wonderland. The few people that were out held onto each other for dear life, tottering along madly, as if on invisible skates, heading for Underground stations.

The car drove through Trafalgar Square, heading on to Whitehall and charging towards Parliament Square, and all the while Posie was desperately willing herself to remain calm in the face of whatever potential danger might lie ahead for her, or for Richard.

She found comfort in running her fingers across the worn, much-loved surface of her old embroidered carpet bag, feeling the lumps and bumps of her familiar things kept inside it: her money-clip, her usual silver notepad and pen, a travel-sized bottle of Parma Violet perfume, a few pieces of make-up and – *what on earth was that?* – a new, alien item felt heavy in Posie's hands; a strange shape, odd somehow.

A gun?

In a tearing hurry, Posie was ripping apart the poppers of the opening of the carpet bag, fumbling in the inside cream-linen pocket of the lining. And sure enough: there it was.

Yes. A gun.

She'd recognise this one anywhere. It belonged to Rufus, Earl of Cardigeon: Posie was sure of it. It was a Webley, a Mark VI revolver, a 1915 model. Standard army provision in the Great War, given to all serving British Officers. Posie had seen Rufus use this gun to frightening effect before, on at least a couple of occasions.

The rising panic and the flurry of butterflies in her stomach now gave way to something else: a solid, calm feeling. *But why?*

Posie, who had always been proud to say she had never had to shoot anyone – certainly never *kill* anyone – in her whole life, was not someone who set great store by violence, or by the threat of violence. But maybe this was the way it *had* to be today?

Posie lay her slim fingers over the heavy weight of the Webley, closing them around the trigger and feeling the certainty of its power within her palm. Whatever had led Dolly Cardigeon to steal her husband's gun and then place it in Posie's old bag and bring the entire lot along with her today, didn't bear pondering right now.

It was enough to know that Posie had it with her. *If* she needed it.

'Here we are, Miss!' chirped the driver, cheerily. 'New Scotland Yard.'

They sped through the double-arched stone entrance with its triple-headed lampposts on each side and swung into a snow-encrusted courtyard in front of the magnificent red-brick building which housed the most important police headquarters in the land.

The entire building rose up splendidly before them, with its snow-capped grey-slate roofs and its many high turrets. It looked deceptively like a fairy-tale castle, rather than a place of investigation and incarceration. The white bands running horizontally around the red turrets and main body of the buildings had always made Posie think of sticks of peppermint Brighton Rock; the sort of thing one bought on holiday as a souvenir.

'Don't wait for me, driver,' instructed Posie, feeling more certain than she felt. 'I'll get a motor-taxi back. I don't know how long I'll be, or where I'll be going next...'

And then, pulling up her veil and her train behind her as best she could, she ran up the grey front steps and she was inside the main reception hall. It was always a depressing place, but today it seemed strangely unstaffed; the waiting room completely unoccupied for once.

'Hello? Anyone about?'

But no-one replied.

Where the Duty Sergeant should have been, at his olive-painted cubby-hole of a room, all was eerily quiet, although the electric lamps burned brightly in the now-dim afternoon light. The telephone apparatus rang out on the desk, again and again, but there was no-one to answer it. Another telephone started ringing far off, somewhere in the deep bowels of the building. A scent of roses – *her* roses – pervaded the place, lacing through the usual institutional stink of bleach and sweat and fear.

Posie knew the place well, of course. Didn't need to follow the signs with arrows stating: 'CHIEF COMMISSIONER'S OFFICE THIS WAY.'

She headed through the corridors which led away from the reception, starting to climb the brown-painted spiral stairs. Going around and around up seven flights, up to where Richard Lovelace's office was situated in a prime position in the very top of one of the towers.

A river runs by, and time rings high.

Well: this line was true enough. Richard's office had a bird's-eye view out across the River Thames with the mooring station of Westminster Pier – with its collection of jolly green-painted huts and its several piers – right below it. If you looked further out you could see Big Ben.

This *must* be what the note had referred to: this office *must* be where Richard was imprisoned.

Posie's steps echoed round and round, and she had to stop once or twice, almost out of breath. She'd coiled up the train of the wedding gown into a sort of loop over one arm by now, and she was aware that the hem of her skirts were covered in a grey dust and filthy cobwebby grime. But she couldn't be bothered to worry about *that*.

She must make quite a sight, Posie thought to herself ironically: huffing and puffing up the stairs, a huge carpet bag in one hand, dressed up to the nines in a wedding dress and veil.

And here was Richard's office, thank goodness.

The frosted-glass windowpane in the top of the door carried the gold-embossed words 'CHIEF COMMISSIONER'.

Posie paused for breath outside.

Her heart beating so loudly she thought it must surely give her away, Posie listened carefully at the doorway, while keeping her head away from the glass windowpane, so she couldn't be seen by anybody inside.

But there was not a sound.

Just a deathly silence.

Trembling, she found herself ripping off her beautiful gossamer-thin silk veil and skull-cap and flinging it all into a corner of the corridor. It was more of a hindrance than a help here. She grabbed up armfuls of the beautiful dress, hitching it up about herself, so her legs were completely free to run, if necessary. She dug into the carpet bag and took out the Webley, tucking it into her sleeve. She threw the bag and the rest of its contents into the corner alongside her veil.

It was now or never.

Chest heaving, fear engulfing every particle of her being, she put a hand briskly on the door handle and then forced it down quickly.

It gave; it was not locked. She opened the door in one easy, flying arc of movement and stepped inside. She found she had pulled out the revolver and was pointing it straight ahead of herself, taking in the whole room and all it contained in one glance.

Oh, Richard. Be here, and be safe.

Alive.

But what she saw was – nothing.

It was fairly dark in the room but she could make out that Richard's desk with its green-glassed reading lamp was empty.

The leather-burnished sofa in the corner with its matching club-like coffee table and an array of newspapers and magazines for visiting guests was also empty. The alcove in the corner by the window with its bookcases and maps and big boardroom-style table was also completely empty.

Nothing.

The venetian-type blinds on all four of the office windows were closed. And Posie stepped forward, not putting the gun down for one second, pulling at each blind and letting it fly noisily upwards, filling the room with the peculiar December snow-diffused afternoon light.

But there was still nothing.

There was no secret place in this turret-room: no place

to hide; no place to hide a body. Posie checked under the desk, under the table, but everything was as it should be. She backed herself against a wall, felt the cold cream-painted surface through the thin silk of her wedding dress. She breathed slowly, exhaled the anguish, the pain, the searing misery, the disappointment. Still, she held onto the Webley, as if for dear life. And then she saw it.

A note on Richard's desk.

A cream piece of paper attached by a piece of sticky tape to the back of his smart Underwood typewriter which always sat squarely in the middle of his bare desk. She should have seen it when she first walked in, but she'd been too busy looking for *him*.

Posie could read it from here. The writing was very large, in green ink. It was definitely Richard's writing; that familiar round, cursive handwriting she knew very well.

But something started to nag at Posie: *Richard never used green ink*. Actually, she had never known him write anything, or sign his name in anything other than Waterman's Royal Blue. There was a bottle of the usual blue ink on his desk right now in fact, together with blotting paper and his fountain pen. *So why use green ink? Where was the green ink kept?*

The note read:

You just missed me. I'm down by the river, Westminster Pier, Number 2.

Sincerely,

R.L.

Posie re-read this several times.

There was much about it which was wrong. In all the time they had known each other, even before they had become engaged, she had never seen her fiancé sign himself 'R.L.' and even in their working-only relationship days, Richard Lovelace had never been cold enough to sign himself off as 'Sincerely'. He was not that type of man. He had always been more affectionate, unusually so.

And that green ink…

No.

Richard had obviously been forced to write this – perhaps at gunpoint? – and then dragged off down to Westminster Pier which was right outside New Scotland Yard, on the Victoria Embankment, below. These piers were mostly used for tourist boats in the summer, for sightseeing tours, and for the occasional barge to moor up at. But in all of their acquaintance Posie had never known Richard once take a boat from here, despite the close proximity of the pier to his office. Not voluntarily.

Richard was not a water sort of person. In fact, he had told her that on several occasions he had become terribly sick when out on the open sea or on the Thames. So this had not been his idea, or his choice of *rendezvous*.

Posie shivered, despite herself. Gathering her wits about her, she stepped briskly out of the office, picked her things up off the dirty floor, then ran as fast as she could down the spiral staircase.

Downstairs, all was still quiet, but she thought she could hear the revving of a motor-car, perhaps drawing up outside the front of the building. Was that the sound of a clatter of footsteps, far off? Perhaps Chief Inspector Oats?

But sensing that time was of the essence, Posie turned away from reception and the entrance she had come in by, and turned to the back of the building, running as fast as she could in her heeled Mary-Janes.

She passed the row of cells, which were completely unoccupied, hurrying down into the dim, gloomy basement where she knew there was an exit onto the small, narrow back lawn of New Scotland Yard, with its private tunnel to the Victoria Embankment and the piers themselves.

The doors to the gardens were all bolted, but mercifully not locked, and Posie flung the bolts back quickly, pushing the doors wide open, running down concrete snow-covered steps onto a scrubby gravelled yard, then into a garden covered in a glimmeringly untouched white carpet. Posie was almost blinded by the whiteness of everything up ahead. Snow was still falling, but much heavier now. It was like being in a blizzard.

Through the falling snowflakes Posie saw the outline of an iron-railed fence and the tall, spiky, dark-black silhouettes of the winter trees lining the Embankment. She saw the road beyond with its sparse traffic, and a thin, flat strip of the silver river further on. A twinkling line of fairy lights hung through the trees like diamond garlands, shining out through the gloom, and a red flashing beacon was straight up ahead, indicating the location of Westminster Pier. The red light flashed on and on. A repeated warning. Over and over.

DANGER HERE.

Was the mooring-station even open? Maybe with all the snow everything had closed down? Including the piers?

So where was Richard now, then? When had he written that strange little note?

The entrance to the small private tunnel leading beneath the road – which belonged exclusively to Scotland Yard – loomed.

Posie breathed hard, summoning all her courage, holding onto her gun, and ran through it in something like a blind panic.

But her fears were groundless. The tunnel was quite empty.

Coming out onto the snow-covered platform of the mooring-station itself she tucked the gun inside her sleeve again and looked about.

Posie saw that the place was obviously still open, despite the worsening weather and the flashing red beacon.

Some black-suited men stood about in the shelter of a shuttered-up green-painted hut which had a sign on its roof stating 'ICES AND TEAS AND FANCY CANDIES SOLD HERE'. They were clustered together and smoking, their bowler hats pulled down well over their ears, against the cold.

Two of the men, one much smaller and older than the other, were laughing together and there was something about the older man which seemed strangely familiar to Posie, but she simply couldn't place him.

A single large black-painted barge was tethered at one of the piers, and about twenty men in beige work overalls were unloading sacks from it. Sacks of something heavy. Posie saw how the men on the barge were working in efficient lines, with other men collecting the sacks from the platform, bringing the goods to waiting cars up on the Victoria Embankment.

Posie looked about her for Pier Number 2.

She was watching for Richard, of course, but watching too for anyone who was paying special regard to her. But no-one had so much as looked in her direction so far.

She had been sure she would be conspicuous in all her fancy finery, but in the flurry of snow blowing around her, Posie's wedding gown was like a helpful invisibility cloak. She was like a ghost; some kind of nothingness to which these busy men around her paid scant regard.

The falling snow had the effect of deadening all the noise, too, and her step had gone unnoticed. The platform moved slightly, bobbing up and down with the choppy tide of the river which, viewed from here, seemed suddenly ridiculously large and wide and deep. Posie felt a wave of nausea rise inside her.

Where was Richard?

She saw that Pier Number 2 was actually the one at which the black barge was moored. Posie stepped closer to it.

No-one was looking at her as the chain of work continued. The men on the barge seemed to be talking to one another in the soft, guttural tongues of another language, and she looked across at the name of the boat, at the fancy yellow letters entwined with red roses on a black, shining background.

THE MARGUERITE – ROTTERDAM.

The barge was Dutch.

Posie saw now that there were crates upon crates of plant bulbs being unloaded, tulip bulbs perhaps, or hyacinths, ready for sale at the London markets for Christmas and January. This was about the right time of year for planting bulbs, wasn't it? There must be thousands of bulbs, worth a fortune, probably.

Posie stepped forward gingerly, the scent of packed, cold earth meeting her nostrils. Aware of the Webley still tucked inside her lace-embroidered sleeve, she cast about for someone in charge, someone from the London Port Authority, perhaps? An official?

But she could see nobody of any such a description. Posie moved closer to the barge, right to its edge.

And then she gasped as she heard her name called out behind her, from way behind the Pier, from the entrance of Scotland Yard's own tunnel, in the gardens across the road.

She turned and stared, shielding her eyes against the brightness.

'Miss Parker! Miss Parker!'

It was Chief Inspector Oats, his face full of panic, his arms waving wildly. 'Come back! Now! They've got–'

And then she heard a rally of gunshots, the staccato reverberations of the gunfire, and she saw Inspector Oats disappear from view.

* * * *

Seven

It happened very suddenly. Posie was aware of something hard being forced into her back, right between her shoulder-blades. Was that the barrel of a gun felt through the thin wedding dress silk?

'Don't move, Miss Parker. Or you'll be sorry. Relax. Didn't you get my message? This is going to be the happiest day of your life.'

A familiar voice, surely?

She didn't have time to feel scared, as suddenly Posie was being dragged backwards and there were several hands pulling her across metal and over coils of ropes.

Downwards.

She smelt the pungent stink of engine-oil and fresh earth, the salty tang of the age-old tides of the river. She was onboard *The Marguerite*. On the open deck.

All about her she saw the snow coming down full-pelt; there was no cover here. It fell on her set-that-morning hair, nestling on her head like an inappropriate halo.

She could still see Scotland Yard's turrets and towers rising up like something sacred in front of her, the twinkling lights of the Embankment. Nearer at hand, she thought she saw Inspector Oats' dark police dress cap appear and then disappear behind a wall.

Suddenly she sensed that nobody was holding onto her anymore, and the pressure at her back had eased. She turned away from looking at the Embankment and spun to face her captor.

And then it all made perfect, horrible sense.

Posie held herself tightly, willing herself not to call out or gasp in surprise, although the shock was enough to almost send her reeling.

For she was looking at the face of a dead man, albeit a man who had been at her aborted wedding ceremony just an hour before, albeit in disguise.

But now she saw right through that disguise.

It was suddenly stripped away, pared back, like scales falling from her eyes. Even though he had not taken off a single part of that clever costume.

It was the flat-footed Reverend Gibbons.

Although, as Posie now knew, it was not the Reverend Jimmy Gibbons at all. Such a man did not exist. And the strange note delivered to Scotland Yard along with all her white roses had been a red herring which had worked a treat.

The whole notion of getting Posie to dash across London through the snow, to a helpless Richard Lovelace imprisoned in his office, had been a complete fiction of the best possible kind.

It seemed more than likely now – as Posie realised in a frightening burst of clarity – that Richard Lovelace had been nowhere near his office today. It had been an effective ruse. Something Posie had fallen for: hook, line and sinker.

How had any of this even been possible?

An old saying of Posie's father's was reverberating annoyingly around her head: *where there is a will, there is a way*.

Well: the will was strong in this case.

And if you wanted to scupper a wedding badly enough, of course you could do it. Posie and Richard's ceremony had been announced, albeit with short notice, in a couple of the national newspapers, and there had been a feature about it in that week's *The Lady*. A bit of careful forward planning was all it took. A couple of well-positioned colleagues, and a couple of good disguises. The best that money could buy. And money was no object here.

Not at all.

For standing in front of Posie was one of the world's most talented, and richest, and most dangerous criminals.

A nasty piece of work through and through. A master criminal who had managed to lie low for the best part of a year-and-a-half, since his last confirmed sighting, while the whole of the international police community had signed him off as being dead.

This was Count Caspian della Rosa. In the flesh.

Posie stared at him now, this short, tubby man on the same eye-level as herself.

She forced herself not to show her fear, although her heart was beating crazily and she had to hold her hands together, fingers interlaced, to stop herself from shaking uncontrollably.

The Count laughed and reached up to his eyes with a strange, dramatic gesture. The sad, heavy-lidded, creased eyes of the Reverend Gibbons were revealed now to be the result of some clever rubber prosthetic lids, and he was tearing these eyepieces off with a single sickening ripping sound.

The round, brown, dog-like eyes of the Caspian della Rosa which she knew of old now stared back at her, keen and sparkling behind the thick round gold spectacles he didn't need. The Count tore these off now, too, as he did his thick, brown, curly wig. He threw all of these things overboard, into the choppy waters of the Thames.

Beneath the wig, Posie saw that the Count was wearing his hair very short, almost shaved off completely. It was a look which did not suit him. Snow fell on his almost-bald scalp and on his bland, potato-like face.

Caspian della Rosa had an aptitude for disguises unparalleled and unsurpassed by any other. In another life, he would have made a perfect character actor, and when Posie had first encountered this truly devilish man on her very first professional outing almost four years ago, he had managed to saunter right under her nose on four or five occasions, every time in a different disguise, every time undetected. It had been a bitter pill to swallow at the time. And Posie had vowed never to let that happen to her again.

But it *had* happened again, hadn't it? In the worst sort of way.

How could she have been such a little fool?

In her nerves, she had not seen through his disguise today, at the altar. Posie had not thought enough to pick apart his story about being a 'locum priest'. Where on earth *was* Father Hoffman? Was he safe? Was he together with Richard?

As if he could read her thoughts, Caspian della Rosa laughed unabashedly, and when he spoke it was not with the English voice of the Reverend Gibbons, but with his own slightly-accented foreign accent. For Caspian della Rosa was Swiss.

'Posie Parker, we meet again. And what a special occasion! You are wondering how I did it, no? But have no fear: that little old priest is just fine, although temporarily indisposed. As is your fiancé, and his trusty little pal who ran around with him in the slippy mud of Flanders.'

'You mean Mr Brown?' Posie frowned, blinking away snow from her eyelashes. 'Rhoddy Brown? What are you talking about?'

And suddenly, all in an instant, Posie saw how clever the man in front of her had been. Or what a piece of luck he had been handed.

For Rhoddy Brown, Richard Lovelace's old colleague from the trenches, had never actually met Posie before. His wife's health had always prevented it. The Mr Brown Posie had encountered today at the Swiss Church had indeed been new to her, but she had not questioned him at all. Had accepted his authenticity. He had been Welsh, and Posie had simply assumed he was who he said he was.

But he had been a fake.

Now she understood it all.

How the evening out at Kettner's which had been described so breezily had probably never happened. It had always seemed unlikely that Richard would have gone out for a dinner the night before his wedding without inviting his usual, trusty police comrades. And so the dancing in a Soho club and the goodbyes at Leicester Square were all now revealed as a fiction.

But Richard *had* been seen this morning at the hotel, at The Montague; that much was real, and Posie held onto that fact like some kind of talisman.

Was it possible that Rhoddy Brown had been staying at the same hotel, a treat from Richard, and that both men had been intercepted on false pretences by Caspian della Rosa and his lackeys at eleven o'clock this morning? That strange telephone call to Richard's room? Had the real Rhoddy Brown been with Richard earlier that morning, as observed by the receptionist?

The man pretending to be Rhoddy Brown must have been brought in specially for the occasion. Brought in to sound genuine, to sound Welsh. He was a jolly good actor, too.

Because when plans had gone slightly awry, and one of their prisoners had managed to make a noise in the church, the fake 'Rhoddy Brown' had acted convincingly, even pretending to help tear down the cupboard by the apse. When in all likelihood, it had been a fake cupboard wall inserted in that doorway by Caspian della Rosa's men this morning, after the priest – and Richard and the real Rhoddy Brown? – had been sealed up inside it.

The Count smiled gleefully.

'You made it so easy for me, Posie dear! Those wedding notices in the newspaper! And then all I had to do was slink in with some of my men yesterday and take a few measurements for that cupboard, for the fake shelves. And the Swiss Church, too! What a perfect touch! So nice of you! I felt so very much at home; on my own turf. All I needed to do earlier this morning was shimmy into the building and chat to that very pleasant Swiss priest, Hoffman. It was the work of a moment to put him out with some chloroform and to hide him… and then my men who had been hiding in the alleyway behind the church just had to switch the flowers, and don their disguises, mostly as policemen, and wait for your nice little Inspector to arrive. I called him myself, you know, at almost eleven o'clock, from the church itself. I pretended to be Father Hoffman; said *you* were at the church with me, having second thoughts about the whole thing! Poor little policeman, he must have run the whole way over. He arrived within minutes. Ah, bless! What devotion! All for nothing!'

'Where's Richard?' Posie asked, trying not to let desperation tinge her voice. This was awful; absolutely rotten. For poor Richard to believe she hadn't wanted to go through with it… It beggared belief.

'Where is the real Rhoddy Brown? Are they in that cupboard in the church? You didn't bargain on one of them making all that noise, did you?'

Caspian della Rosa laughed again. 'Have no fear. Both are still alive. For now…'

Posie was suddenly aware of a distinct noise, a growling and rumbling beneath her, an engine-like sound coming up from somewhere deep within the barge she was standing upon. The stink of fuel was rising to her nostrils, making her gag.

'We'll shortly be leaving, Posie. Say goodbye to London. To all of this. Forever.'

Caspian della Rosa had now ripped off his black-and-white vestments, which seemed, as with so much else of his performance today, to be of the purest theatrical variety. They slipped to the floor with no weight at all. Below these he wore an immaculately-tailored blue pinstripe suit, with a pink cravat and matching pocket-handkerchief. Posie saw a quick flash of shining metal in the air and realised it was the black-and-gold cane she had watched the priest walk away with earlier, tapping his way securely through the snow, supposedly on his way to preside over another wedding. The Count was fingering the end of the cane.

Nothing about the man in front of her was to be trusted, or taken at face-value.

Was this object actually something else masquerading as a cane? Something dangerous? Was this what Posie had felt at her back? So far there didn't seem to be an actual gun anywhere on the Count's own person. Which was *something*. The gunfire must have been the work of one of the Count's men…

Posie remembered back to the very last day of 1921, three years ago, at the end of a long and complicated investigation. How the crazy criminal mastermind in front of her had tried to kidnap her then; to take her away, again by water, off to some European dream of the future of his – a drug-financed future – where everything was underpinned by crime. He had wanted Posie to become his partner, his wife. He had admitted to an obsessive love for her back then. A love which knew no bounds, had no safety checks.

She had got out of that situation by the skin of her teeth.

Caspian della Rosa had reappeared again in 1923, but slightly less alarmingly: part of a big shoot-out which he had obviously hoped would provide a cover for stealing away with Posie, but which had ended badly for him. He had been very seriously wounded but was dragged off by a supremely loyal employee, with most of the international police community declaring the Count as being dead.

And now, on the point of stepping into an altogether different destiny, a future with Richard Lovelace, it seemed Posie would need to extract herself from this current hot mess.

All of her life, Posie had been tenacious. She'd been a survivor. The last few years she'd been pretty much on her own.

Finally, she was on the brink of happiness, on the brink of forging a future with a man she loved, with a ready-made family of children, and with the promise of a child of their own to seal the union. How could she let Caspian della Rosa steal this future away from her now?

No: she would not let that happen.

Posie sensed the furtive movements of several men in beige overalls around her, scurrying about, making fast equipment, pulling at ropes and battening down hatches.

'Step this way, please, Posie.' The Count smiled, indicating towards an open trapdoor in the deck, with a ladder leading down into an uninviting semi-darkness. 'We have a long journey ahead of us. I must say, you're looking more than usually lovely today. You'll be pleased to know that your beautiful gown is not for nothing. It won't be wasted. One of the chaps onboard is a fully-certified priest. You've met him before, actually. Today. Although he was pretending to be an Organist.'

Posie gasped. The Organist had been a fake, too?

But that fitted: in fact, the older man standing on the Pier just now had seemed familiar to her. Unplaceable. That had surely been the Organist? He, together with the younger man 'playing' Brown, together with goodness only knew who, must have hurtled across London right behind Posie in a series of cars to ensure they made this boat…

She tried to marshal her thoughts. '*Sorry?* A priest, you say? To do what, exactly?'

'Why, Posie! What a question! To marry us in an instant, of course. You and me. As soon as we get out to sea, into international waters.'

'Marry? Marry *you*?'

'Of course. That is what this is all about, of course. I wanted to marry you back in 1921, and that hasn't changed a bit. All these years, lurking and hiding, that one thought spurred me on. Kept me going. I wasn't going to have you marry another, was I? You forced me into action, my dear. Forced me to break cover. But as it turned out it was all rather fun. And profitable. Imagine what sort of team we will be. You have nothing to fear from me, my darling. You'll want for nothing. Your whole future will be like a dream.'

A dream?

'A bad dream,' breathed Posie under her breath. But she was sensible enough not to say anything to anger the Count aloud: he had a famously terrible temper and she had seen his anger in action before.

She whipped around and saw that a Dutchman was untying one of the thick ropes tethering *The Marguerite* to the Pier.

Another man, but this one in a black overcoat and cap, was clambering up out of the trapdoor to see what was happening, checking his watch. Posie saw a flash of red hair beneath the cap and recognised him immediately as the man who had pretended to be Rhoddy Brown, and when he saw her astonishment, he grinned broadly at her and gave a mock salute before vanishing again.

'Posie? Now, darling... below deck?'

Several men onboard were shouting. Ropes were being slipped through knots, and a London Port Authority Official had suddenly appeared on the pier beside the boat waving paperwork at the Count:

'Is this your vessel, sir? You can't sail out in this weather! That's why the red light is flashing! Do you see it? Are you crazy? I tell you: you can't leave here. Lives will be put at risk...'

And here was Chief Inspector Oats again, right behind the Port Official, his eyes darting from side to side, taking in Posie in her white dress, assessing the situation, the fast-falling snow, the danger at every turn.

Caspian della Rosa had that cane out still, was tweaking it and spinning it slightly...

Posie had never pulled a gun on anybody in her entire life.

But that didn't mean things couldn't change. This was her wedding day. An extraordinary day, after all.

She turned to call out to Oats, but really she was creating a distraction, pulling out the hidden Webley from her lace sleeve, swirling around and facing Caspian della Rosa full-on.

Posie had her finger tight on the trigger. She was mindful of being freezing cold, impossibly so, but her hands were steady and she didn't tremble once. *Could she really be doing this?*

But she could do anything. If she had to.

Mindful of her own life, and her safety, but possibly more for the future of the life she knew she carried inside her, she turned to face her nemesis. He'd raised his eyebrows, completely surprised, wrong-footed, somehow.

But she'd paused a moment too long: given him too much time. In that moment of warning he'd raised the cane, and the gold lid was flicked off, revealing a lethal-looking golden dart within, sharp as you like.

Caspian della Rosa had stepped back slightly and now they faced each other, Posie and her would-be suitor, equally matched in the falling snow. It was an impasse. A stalemate.

'Put down that gun. Nicely now, Posie darling. Let's all be friendly, shall we? We're going to leave now, ride away, without any more of this silly farce. Hand me your fancy little gun, will you? I don't want to hurt you: really, I don't. And this special Japanese dart based on the ancient "Tofugu" design: it's poisonous, you know. Absolutely lethal. I don't really want to shoot you with it, or the stupid-looking policeman, or this official here. So darling, play nicely.'

Caspian della Rosa was calm, friendly almost. But there was something crazed in those brown eyes and behind that fat-lipped smile which unnerved Posie. *Where could this end?*

She kept eye-contact with her captor, did her best to smile trustingly, and then started to bring the Webley down, moving it as if she was going to cradle it in both hands before passing it over, in her open palms, like an offering. The Count moved as if to take it from her.

All of my life was not destined to end here, at this point, right now, Posie thought to herself bitterly. And anger drove her on.

I will not end up with this dreadful, conceited, criminal little podge of a man.

Before she passed the Webley across, Posie snapped the trigger tight with her right hand, aimed and shot twice into the fleshy part of Caspian della Rosa's right thigh, the bullets embedding themselves nicely inside.

An unearthly scream filled the air, caught and muffled by the snow. Men all around were ducking and crouching, fearing reprisals, Oats included.

But reprisals didn't come.

Posie watched as in the span of a single second the Count crumpled in a wild, tumbling arc onto the deck of his own boat. A sagging mess. At the same time, probably accidentally, he shot the gold-tipped dart from its casing, and Posie saw it fly heavenwards, uselessly, futilely, ready to cause no more pain than to end up in the sludge of the bottom of the River Thames.

Caspian della Rosa was writhing in pain, and dark smeary tar-like blood was coursing out from him over the slippery, snow-clad decking of the barge, blotting its way through the powder of the icing-sugar-like snow, reaching to the edge of Posie's white silk gown.

She knew, if her aim had been right, that his injuries would not be life-threatening. She had got to the weary point where she had no remorse. Besides, it served Caspian della Rosa bally well right.

Posie tried not to look at him too much.

And suddenly they were surrounded by scores of Dutch bargemen, and the London Port Official, and Inspector Oats, all scrabbling around the injured man, who was making small whining noises every now and again.

'I'll call an ambulance,' shouted the Port Official and ran towards one of the green huts on the pier. The bargemen were wild-eyed and nervy, seeking for directions among themselves, not knowing what to do next, as if they were in some live trap. Looking for a Deputy.

Posie scanned the deck. For surely Caspian della Rosa's Deputy was the fake Rhoddy Brown? Or the Organist? Or both of them? Why didn't *they* come up here and make themselves known?

Posie saw how the bargemen were nodding towards the hold of the barge, how their faces were set and angry. And then they were staring with a mixture of disgust and fear towards Chief Inspector Oats himself, taking in his police insignia. They were downright scared.

Guilty...

'Oh! I see! How clever!'

For wouldn't it have made sense that Caspian della Rosa would have come to London not just to take home Posie as some sort of prize, but also to *do* something wildly criminal at the same time? To make vast amounts of money, to continue managing his empire? *Two birds:*

one stone. He himself had used the word 'profitable' about today's activities.

Posie wanted to laugh suddenly, completely inappropriately.

Out of the corner of her eye she saw a small blue rubber dinghy, carrying a couple of crew members in black overcoats and caps, pushing off from the front of the barge, heading out up river in the whirling snow.

There go the deputies…

Inspector Oats was looking at Posie with some concern. Unusually, for him. He was taking off his navy-blue-and-gold-encrusted jacket, quickly throwing it over Posie's shoulders. She realised suddenly that she was beyond the point of being freezing cold.

Oats coughed softly: 'He's fine, Miss. I've spoken to him on the telephone. Your Richard was bound and gagged and hidden up in the Organist's balcony, together with the real Organist. He was there all the time and heard the whole thing! His pal Rhoddy was walled up with the old priest. What a mare's nest! After we left the church, Count della Rosa's accomplices caused a debacle by shooting up into the air, then they made a run for it, locking everyone inside. None of the congregation could get out, despite your having directed people to go and eat the Wedding Breakfast. The church was eventually unlocked by one of the journalists I couldn't manage to shoo away. You know how persistent they are… sell their souls for a story. Especially one like today! Are you okay, Miss? You've had quite an ordeal.'

Posie didn't know whether to laugh or cry. 'I'm fine. Completely fine.'

'He's waiting for you still, Miss. At the church, you know. As are all the congregation.'

Posie checked her wristwatch. It was almost three o'clock. She grinned. 'They must all be starving by now.'

'I'll say, Miss.'

She made to leave, but then pointed past the wounded

Caspian della Rosa, to the barge itself. She felt the need to return a favour.

'I think you'll find, Chief Inspector, that if you get some of your men over here now to search this barge, you'll find thousands of pounds worth – if not millions of pounds worth – of drugs hidden within these crates of tulip bulbs. It's a very clever operation, sir. If you can't trace the whole supply and receivership line, at least you will have succeeded in apprehending these men here, and laying claim to the drugs themselves. Quite a productive day, eh?'

And Chief Inspector Oats was suddenly nodding, speaking with the Port Official who had just returned, asking for back-up to come.

But Posie didn't wait for any of this.

Posie hurried off the Pier, climbing the steps to the Embankment itself, with Chief Inspector Oats' jacket still slung about her shoulders. In the distance she heard the familiar CLANG-CLANG of an ambulance on its way.

She cursed the fact she'd sent her wedding car away. She could have done with it now. Posie looked wildly about her and then, as if by magic, far away on the right she saw the yellow twin headlamps of a motor-taxi beetling along towards her.

She stepped onto the kerb and waved it down.

'Endell Street, please. Fast as you can.'

* * * *

Eight

She got back to the Swiss Church in about fifteen minutes. This time the doors were closed, but when she pushed them they opened in front of her, easily.

It was like *déjà vu*.

But this time there was no bouquet in her hands, only the grubby carpet bag, although she had at least managed to fish out the beautiful veil and headdress and reattach them, to stick on a touch more pink lipstick in the motor-taxi and to tidy up her eye-black.

There was no sense of disappointment at the lack of white roses this time, no wonder about who had sent the yellow mimosa. That had all been arranged by Caspian della Rosa, of course. He'd sent mimosa to Posie back in 1921, and again today. Simply because it was his favourite flower. His calling card.

Posie's dress was stained with Dolly's face powder and general London grime and Caspian della Rosa's blood, and she smelt of petrol and tulip bulbs rather than her usual Parma Violet.

She still held the Webley in her hands, and she hadn't got rid of the trembling sensation which had overcome her in the taxi on the way here.

But this time things would be okay.

For here was Richard.

Here he was, that dear man who had promised himself to her, forever, who would never, ever have jilted her at the altar.

Richard Lovelace was wearing his full police dress uniform, and although his face had a white and shocked look about it, with a scratch and a just-appearing blue bruise along the left cheekbone, he didn't seem much the worse for wear. His green eyes lit up when he saw Posie appear in the doorway, and he couldn't stop beaming.

Next to him was Father Hoffman, the priest Posie had met the week before. He was wearing his real vestments, heavy-looking and black and rather crumpled now, but real all the same.

And over on Richard's left, holding a small blue velvet box bearing two fairly cheap gold wedding rings from Woolworths was the man Posie assumed must be the real Rhoddy Brown.

He was as different from the fake, red-haired, chunky Mr Brown from earlier as was possible to be: dark, small, bony-looking, fragile somehow, almost yellow all over. It occurred to Posie that Rhoddy Brown himself was not well, and his ill-health, as well as his wife's, had probably prevented him from coming up to London before.

It was a massive thing that he had come here today for Richard's wedding. There had been no stag-night dinner, of course not. The two old friends had probably had a quiet supper at the hotel bar the evening before. What a dreadful time the poor man must have had this morning, to be accosted and set upon by Caspian della Rosa's gang of men.

Had Rhoddy Brown ever thought he would make it out of London alive, to return to his sick wife? Had he ever questioned his judgement at journeying up from Wales to be here today? Had he thought that this might be *it*?

That all that hardship of getting through the trenches had actually been for nothing?

But now everybody was on their feet. Organ music thundered out suddenly.

Everybody was laughing, clapping, taking no note of the oddness of it all. Especially not Rhoddy Brown, who was grinning widely. It would take much more than all of this disaster to cast him down for long.

Posie saw that the church seemed to be fuller than it had been before, and she realised that the newspaper journalists and photographers who had been waiting outside before, were all now *inside*, packed around the back of the church. Flash-bulbs were suddenly going off and Posie smiled as much as she could manage and tried to compose herself.

But Richard Lovelace was not standing on ceremony.

He strode towards Posie, meeting her halfway down the aisle. He saw the Webley in her hands, and without saying anything he gently took it and placed it in an inside pocket of his dress jacket. Then he took her in a great big bear hug, lifted her clean off the ground, buried his face in her hair. Posie thought he might blub. As might she.

And at that very moment she felt a kick inside.

'Come on,' she hissed at him, grinning. 'We've got a wedding to get on with. Everybody is waiting. Let's just hope it goes ahead this time.'

And then she tucked her hand neatly into Richard's arm, and stepped forward with him, into the future which was waiting for her.

* * * *

EPILOGUE

Later, at the much-delayed Wedding Breakfast, which was really a dinner, Posie had returned the Webley to Dolly, Countess of Cardigeon, whispering her thanks.

'But how on earth did you *know*, Dolly? How did you think to bring a gun to a wedding?'

Dolly had laughed, watching her children misbehave, with their nursemaid pulling her hair out in exasperation. 'With you, Posie love, anythin' is possible, isn't it?'

Dolly had lit a cigarette, and blown a perfect smoke ring as a small jazz band started to play. 'Besides, there's somethin' about weddings which brings out the best in people. And the worst, too. I had it in mind that every lunatic in London might be there at the Swiss Church waitin' for you today. And I was right, wasn't I? The worst kind of lunatic *was* waitin' for you, actually. You certainly attract them, don't you, lovey?'

And much later still, when all the fuss had died down, and speeches had been made, and toasts had been drunk, and dancing had been done, and Rhoddy Brown had been packed off on the train from Paddington to return to Wales with all due haste, Posie – now Mrs Lovelace – and her new husband decided *not* to stay in their fancy wedding suite at The Montague, after all.

They decided to return to what would now be their family home, the top-floor flat in Museum Chambers.

As they entered the flat, the telephone was ringing out shrilly.

It was Chief Inspector Oats with the news that the entire Dutch crew of bargemen had handed themselves in for arrest at Scotland Yard, and a simply massive haul of drugs had been found aboard *The Marguerite*.

The Inspector informed them that Caspian della Rosa had been taken to St Thomas' Hospital nearby, where he had been deemed to be in a serious, but not critical state: the wounds on his leg would heal eventually but it would not be a quick recovery. The Count had been placed on a ward guarded by a team of Scotland Yard's best men.

There was, hopefully, no question of him escaping this time.

The eerily quiet Scotland Yard which Posie had run through that afternoon had been due to the fact that some of Caspian della Rosa's Dutch bargemen had drugged and bound the Duty Sergeant, depositing him safely out of the way in a locked interview room just before Posie had turned up. They had also let out all of the criminals who were locked in the overnight cells, just for a laugh. Some of these criminals had already been tracked down, but many hadn't, and these men were roaming around London, even now.

Chief Inspector Oats was now tasked with the clean-up operation, but the success of the drugs haul had been so considerable, and the praise heaped upon him so great, that he seemed remarkably jaunty considering the fact that he would now have to work non-stop all weekend.

Posie yawned.

She felt tired to the bone.

It was past midnight, and for the first time that day Richard and she were alone together.

They were standing in their light-blue-painted sitting-room. They should have had a bottle of champagne, or something bubbly and intoxicating to celebrate their nuptials with. But they were both too tired, and besides, Posie couldn't drink just now.

They drank Bovril instead.

Posie was wearing a velvet dressing gown in midnight blue, with small gold beads sewn around the edges of the collar and cuffs. It matched her eyes exactly, although it had grown tight across the belly, especially this last week. It wouldn't fit for much longer.

She pressed her face against the coldness of the windowpane, looking down into Museum Street below. The snow was still falling; slight drifts were forming in the dark street and the lanterns outside the British Museum glowed wearily through the strange snowy mist.

Her husband had come up behind her and he had his strong arms around her, his bruised and battered face resting in her black, black hair.

'Things never turn out how we plan them to, do they, Posie?' Richard Lovelace said quietly, bending down a bit to nuzzle her neck.

'But this was truly a spectacular mess! While I was up there on that ruddy balcony today, tied up like a prize Christmas turkey, I could hear everything going on below in the church; everything you said. It was like a living nightmare. I could only imagine what you must have been feeling, my love. As if I had abandoned you! I wanted to scream, but I was gagged so darn effectively. I could have cursed Caspian della Rosa: he'd been so clever, lying in wait and springing out on poor old Rhoddy and me when we'd turned up at the church. You know he telephoned to me in the morning pretending to be the priest? He said you were having doubts about me. About the marriage…'

'*As if!*' spluttered Posie. 'I can't believe you thought for a second I would have doubts!'

'Oh, darling,' Lovelace whispered, almost under his breath, 'I was *terrified* you were backing out. But then I realised what a fool I'd been, falling into his trap so nicely! But it was too bally late. They tied up Rhoddy first and threatened to shoot him if I didn't write that note to you in green ink; some wretched false clue. And then they dragged Rhoddy off, and I was fearful for his life the whole time: you realise he's not a strong man? Although he's a very brave one…'

Richard Lovelace groaned with sadness and regret. 'And I was so helpless. Rhoddy taken off goodness knew where, and *you* were about to fall right into della Rosa's trap, too. And when you left the church, to speed across London like some guardian angel to find me at Scotland Yard…' he swallowed uneasily, 'I thought that would be it. That I'd lost you for good. That Caspian della Rosa would have won. I swear to God I don't know what I would have done.'

'Darling, don't think any more of it. That way madness lies. Caspian della Rosa is not going to trouble us again. By marrying me today you have foiled his plans completely. We have so much to look forward to. And now we belong together. *Properly* I mean.'

Lovelace covered her hands in his, and he found her wedding ring and held onto her very tightly.

'Shall we go to bed, *Mrs* Lovelace?'

'Oh, yes,' said Posie Parker, who had already decided she was going to keep on using her maiden name, but hadn't got around to telling her husband about it yet.

After all, a girl likes to keep some sense of mystery about herself. Something elusive; a sense of drama.

But that discussion could wait for tomorrow.

Besides, there had been quite enough drama for one day.

****

Have you read Posie's eighth adventure,
Murder on the White Cliffs?

(If not read on for a FREE taster...)

MURDER
ON THE
WHITE CLIFFS

A POSIE PARKER MYSTERY #8

L. B. HATHAWAY

WHITEHAVEN

WHITEHAVEN MAN PRESS

London

PROLOGUE

It was too dark, too dangerous, to be out on a night like this. Any fool knew that, and whatever else Elsie Moncrieff was, she was no fool.

But still, here she was.

It was past eleven o'clock, and the November rain lashed down unforgivingly. She was certain that no-one had seen her leave. She'd locked the door of her flat in the staff quarters and walked briskly along the unmade gravel road running parallel to the beach. The tide was out and yet the foaming sea-spray from the breakers was carried on the wind to her in heavy salty slaps across the face.

She'd hurried past the blackness of the 'village' on the beach: past the Bay Bungalow and the holiday cottages, past the Excelsior Tea-Rooms, all catering for fashionable summer visitors; everything now shuttered and sleeping in wintry darkness.

All except the exclusive Bay Hotel.

The Bay Hotel boasted of being open year-round, but it was an exaggeration really. Elsie knew it well: knew they operated only a skeleton staff during November, the most unpopular month. Tonight only a few lights blazed out as she passed. Right in front of the hotel some local lads had built up a great mass of driftwood ready for Bonfire

Night next week, and Elsie carefully stepped around it. Occasionally she turned her flash-light on, just to check where she was going, but she snapped it off again each time, within seconds.

Elsie hadn't bothered with an umbrella, the wind made it impossible. No handbag either. She was wearing head-to-toe black oilskins, and she moved like a shadow through the storm.

A dog barked in the nothingness. The pulsing rays from the South Foreland Lighthouse, located further on towards Dover, did little tonight to break through the darkness. A couple of times Elsie thought she heard something crack behind her, a twig maybe, but when she turned, abruptly each time, she was quite alone. She chided herself momentarily for her nerves.

She'd turned away from the old smugglers pub on the beach, The Green Man, which should have stopped serving at ten o'clock, this being a Sunday, but which was still open.

Elsie hadn't taken the steep road which would lead up to the safety of St Margaret's-at-Cliffe, the village. She turned instead up the sharp precipitous lane which was Beach Road, passing the boarded-up black silhouette of Maypole Manor, heavy in its isolation. She headed on to the very top of the cliff, to Ness Point. Elsie's face was stinging by now, dead-cold, but she barely felt the discomfort.

Her fingers brushed against a piece of paper in her pocket, picked up from her own door-mat as she had left tonight, with her boss's handwriting on it. But she immediately disregarded it. Anything from Petronella Douglas could wait. Could wait forever.

Elsie turned her torch on once she was on the cliff-top, keeping it trained on the ground. She'd arrived at the place.

Here.

A bench.

Placed fairly near the edge of the cliff for the fine views over the English Channel, the bench was set back among a scrabble of gorse and low, twisty trees which had woven a sort of dense canopy over and around the seat, providing a place of safety. But the bench didn't seem quite so safe tonight; the wind whistling, the rain even worse up here on this outcrop.

Elsie was obviously the first to arrive and she flung herself down on the seat, drawing breath, surprised at the effort the fifteen-minute walk had taken out of her.

Where was he?

Had she come to the right place?

Was he, even now, waiting for her elsewhere? The man with whom she had such a connection, to whom she was inextricably bound. The man she had yearned for and keened for these last few months.

The note hadn't mentioned the cliff-top specifically. Nothing about Ness Point at all. It had been short.

The usual spot. Come alone.
Half-past eleven tonight.

The note had come like a bolt out of the blue this morning, totally unexpected. But the timing was perfect. Things were changing here fast.

The darkness, the wind and the rain, the storm all around, this position atop a cliff right at the very edge of England might have unnerved some, caused them to turn and run. But Elsie Moncrieff was tough, tough as you like.

Elsie told herself this now; repeated it like a precious mantra.

Reminded herself how well she had done here: how working at White Shaw in St Margaret's Bay for the famous Fashion House, Douglas & Stone, was a dream job which most women could only ever hope for.

But dreams could become nightmares, couldn't they?

And now Elsie was ready to leave. She just had to hope that her way out remained open.

As she waited for him, she thought how much she had missed him. Her other half. Gracious, a few months ago she had even written to that fancy Private Detective, that woman, Miss Parker: whose knack at solving crimes was equally matched by a photogenic rapport with the British press; whose huge-eyed beauty was often to be found staring out from the pages of newspapers and penny magazines. But Elsie had heard nothing from her by return. Not a dicky bird. Probably for the best, looking back.

And then suddenly the bench seemed to shift underneath her, re-adjust to an added weight.

He was here.

He'd arrived out of the night with no torch, no warning. Just like her, a spirit on the wind.

She'd sensed his presence before she saw him; the lemon tang of him perceptible even through the sea-salt spray. But hang about: there was something else here, wasn't there? Something just tangible. A woman's scent which wasn't natural or subtle.

A *town* perfume. An expensive perfume which Elsie recognised. A few of the women she knew wore it.

So was there a woman here too?

And as she turned to her left in the driving rain she breathed a sigh of relief. He was quite alone. No woman.

She saw from his outline that he was wearing a black oilskin coat with a high, funnel-necked sweater below, like a fisherman. He had a sou'wester hat on his head and he was staring ahead, out to the blackness of the sea. Because she knew him of old, she saw the worry etched in every line of his being.

'Filthy night, isn't it?'

When he spoke she was reminded of her childhood, the language of that time, when she had been a small, pig-tailed girl. The familiarity of it made her feel achingly sad. She was reminded too of the glory days, when they'd worked together so well, before. Nearby. When there had been three of them.

'I didn't mean for us to meet up here in the middle of a storm. It's hardly ideal.'

'No matter. I'd have traipsed through hell and high water to meet you. You know you can trust me.'

He turned to face her at last. 'But can I really, Elise?'

Elise?

She couldn't see his eyes, the bright blue which she knew so well, but she could hear the ice in his voice. Elsie frowned, perched forward on the bench. 'You haven't called me that in years. No-one has. I'm Elsie. Just "Elsie". Shorter, simpler. Better. You know that.'

For a few seconds he didn't answer.

'You were our golden child, Elise. Do you remember your little dolls? Your singing, your dancing. Your opera! You were so talented. Before we were here. Before all of *this*. This mess...'

Something was wrong.

Elsie stared at him in a dawning horror. 'What are you talking about? *What* mess? I've done very well here these last three years, in difficult circumstances. Are you here to tell me I've done something wrong?'

The man didn't answer immediately. But then he made a show of getting to his feet, and he pulled Elsie up with him, their raincoats slipping and sliding as they held on to each other.

'Not you, Elise. But it's a mess all the same. Look, we're in danger. Let's walk, shall we? Somewhere more hospitable. I had the strange idea that I was followed up here; I hope my message to you wasn't intercepted. That pub looked like it was still open. Shall we head there? Who would stop us?'

'*What* danger?' Elsie spat out a hoot of laughter. 'I don't care anyhow. I'm leaving. But I suppose you know that?'

The man stopped, pulled up short, so she nearly bumped right into him. And then came the anger. She shone her torch at him and watched in surprise as his beautiful, sun-tanned, rain-spattered face was riven with fury.

'What's happened to you, Elise? I *know* you wrote to Posie Parker by the way. And missing the all-important event last night? What on earth are you up to?'

'Is that why you contacted me? To scold me?'

He took her by the shoulders, but gently, sadly. 'Of course I'm not here to scold you. You're in danger, Elise: real trouble. We all are. *That's* why I came. I've been close at hand, watching things unfurl. I needed to warn you, if it was the last thing I did.'

'Liar!'

Confusion and anger bubbled over and Elsie shone her torch in his eyes on purpose, blinding him. He grabbed at it and they struggled, grappling together. He won and it went rolling off into the undergrowth somewhere.

'Now look what you've done.' Elsie was on her knees, scrabbling frantically. The flash-light belonged to Tony Stone. Which meant it was expensive: the best of the best. Elsie had borrowed it without asking. And Tony would surely miss it if she didn't manage to retrieve it.

She called out to her companion: 'Help me, won't you?'

And it was just at this moment that Elsie Moncrieff sensed a furtive shadow darting out of the undergrowth, smelt the strong town perfume yet again, and felt a sharp sudden push at the back of her slippery oilskin coat.

A powerful hand.

She yelled out, pointlessly, and then she was rolling, over and over, like a child's rubber ball bouncing down steps. Except these were no steps, and she was no child's plaything.

Terror engulfed her in that split-second, but the urge to survive was stronger, forcing herself to *think*, to *calm down*. In a minute this would all stop.

Someone would save her.

'*Elise!*' she heard him scream from behind her. 'No!'

In a flash she saw him lit up by a beam from the South Foreland Lighthouse along the coast, and she saw he was no longer alone. A woman was beside him, shouting.

Sodden chalk and wet grass and stones and seeping water were slipping past her in a nightmarish blur as her hands clawed at the air, but found no purchase.

And then suddenly she was falling, falling through the air, through a symphony of shadows, hundreds and hundreds of feet downwards.

The White Cliffs she had come to love were rushing past her, and she was engulfed in the roar of the sea below.

And in that nightmarish arc of a disaster Elsie – or *Elise* – heard him screaming up above, and all she knew next was blackness.

* * * *

PART ONE
Bonfire Night
(Tuesday 4th November
to Wednesday 5th
November, 1924)

One

Richard Lovelace, forty-something and handsome in a gingery way, was standing in his shirtsleeves in the hallway of his fiancée's top-floor Bloomsbury flat, supervising a team of men who were carting out box-loads of another man's possessions.

It was taking an age.

At his feet were several tins of Manders' Quick-Dry pink paint in differing shades, ranging from spun-sugar through to fiery salmon, which he suddenly felt like kicking at. The Decorator was having an extended cup of tea in the kitchen, having been directed smartly to get out of the way.

Lovelace groaned at the passing Foreman. 'Dash it all, Smith! Hurry the blazes up, won't you?'

He had tried to stop himself checking his wristwatch every couple of minutes, tried to stop himself looking irritated, but now he cracked. Richard Lovelace was the recently-promoted Chief Commissioner of New Scotland Yard, a sought-after Police Detective whose ready laugh and gentle humour hid a razor-sharp wit and first-class mind. He had an impressive history of catching the capital's most hardened criminals, and he was in the middle of a high-profile case involving a raid on a jewellery shop on Bond Street.

Lovelace really needed to be at his desk right now on this cold November morning, prepping for an important meeting on the Bond Street case, taking place in one hour's time. Not here.

But his fiancée was Posie Parker, London's premier female Private Detective, and he loved her more than life itself. He'd have done anything for her. Quite literally. They were getting married soon and all this hanging around was part of *that*: the plan to have a future together.

It had been obvious to Lovelace when he proposed marriage to Posie four months previously that she would never in a million years agree to move to his suburban home in Clapham where he and his toddler daughter, Phyllis, resided. Posie would have to be dragged kicking and screaming out of her beloved Museum Chambers flat first, and that was no way to begin a marriage, was it?

So he'd tentatively suggested that they all move in *here* with Posie. It had been the only thing he could think of. And Posie had agreed readily, happily. Probably out of sheer relief that she didn't have to move, Richard Lovelace now thought.

The Bloomsbury flat was definitely big enough: four bedrooms, a large lounge, a modern kitchen, a nice central location, right next to the British Museum, with the shops and schools of Holborn and Covent Garden on the doorstep. It *needed* to be big enough: not only was there himself and Phyllis to move in immediately after the wedding, but there was also the small matter of Richard's Russian Housekeeper, Masha, and a waif-and-stray orphan baby, born very small and sickly, named Katie, whom Lovelace had adopted during the summertime and who would also need to move in with them when she was eventually discharged from Great Ormond Street, the hospital which had been expertly looking after her.

The wedding had been roughly pencilled in for Christmas-time. And this place had to be made ready first.

Rooms cleared. Re-decorated. One room in particular.

In Posie's not-so-distant past she had been the high-profile partner of Alaric Boynton-Dale, the celebrated Explorer: a glamorous and aristocratic adventurer whose exploits and dashing good looks had captured the hearts and minds of the nation. Whose death a year ago while abroad had caused outpourings of grief and filled column after column in the British newspapers.

Alaric had 'lodged' with Posie for more than a year, keeping a self-contained bedroom in her flat, rent-free, for using in between his expeditions. When he had died, Posie had locked his door, and the room hadn't been opened up again until this morning. And now crates of Alaric's clothes and rugs and maps were all being carried away, bound for the Royal Geographical Society in South Kensington, to whom Alaric had bequeathed all of his personal belongings on death.

This big job of clearing Alaric's messy room – which was essentially a beautiful and huge light-filled space with a stunning view over the London skyline – had been in Richard and Posie's diary for ages. The removal men had been booked and paid for, the Royal Geographical Society ready and waiting to start sorting through Alaric's treasures, the Decorator paid in advance.

Together they had decided that Alaric's old room would become the new nursery. A big room for Phyllis and Katie to share. There was even a small adjoining room which would perfectly suit Masha. A lick of pink paint and some sturdy child-proof iron bars at the window was all that was needed. And a trip to Gamages on High Holborn to buy some beautiful new toys to make it seem fresh and inviting: a compensation for Phyllis who was trading in her old home with its familiarity and its garden, neither of which she would have at Museum Chambers.

Simple.

Plain sailing.

Only of course it wasn't.

Lovelace glanced around at Posie's beautiful pale-green living room, with its expensive dark-wood drinks cabinet and framed hieroglyphs hung above the fireplace. He remembered that this was where they'd been when they'd discussed it all; planning things out, two months back. He frowned now at the memory.

It had been an August evening, but the air had already grown chilly and was smelling of autumn, the fire had been lit and was throwing flickers of shadows up the walls. Rare time alone for them, without Phyllis. The sofa which held them both like a strong ship seemed alone and rudderless on a candle-lit sea.

Posie had been on his lap, in his arms, the silk of her gown fluid against the roughness of his stubble, the scent of her Parma Violet perfume heavy in the air between them.

He'd been anxious about the move to Museum Chambers. And he'd said so.

'But Posie, are you sure it's not going to be too much of an intrusion? This place is beautiful. It's so very *you*.'

'And now it will be so very *us*. All of us. You; me; the girls; Masha. I'll even put the fancy glassware away if it worries you. We can re-do this room, make it special for *us*.'

'No, dearest one. No.'

'I insist, Richard. We'll choose the colour of the walls together. Anything other than pale green, eh? I'll put those hieroglyphs into storage and we'll buy new decorations in the new deco style. Or maybe we'll just have a great big wedding picture of us up there in its place instead? Darling love, please stop looking so worried about it all. That beautiful red hair of yours will all turn grey in an instant and then I'll feel terribly guilty.'

But before she could reach her mouth to his and cover his dear, familiar face with a hundred kisses, he said it:

'And Alaric's room? Will you open it up or will I? It's obviously something of a Pandora's Box for you, darling, and no wonder. But it seems to me the sooner it's dealt with, the better.'

Posie had nodded slowly. 'Absolutely. It's been laziness, really. It's quite time. You book the men and I'll just let them take everything in one go. I'll oversee it. We might as well paint the walls at the same time. Don't you think? We'll be nice and efficient.'

And then had come that tide of longed-for kisses and he'd given himself up to her at last – couldn't resist, just this once – and then he'd booked the removal men and the Decorator, forgetting about it all until late yesterday afternoon.

And then – yesterday – the plans for today's flat clearance had been abruptly changed.

They'd met in his office at New Scotland Yard – a new office, bigger, as befitted his new status, with a view out across the street-lights of the Embankment and the Thames – with Posie turning up unexpectedly at four o'clock, bounding in, clutching at a newspaper, looking wildly excited. Feverish almost, under the unbecoming pea-green shades of the institutional glass lamps.

Lovelace had groaned inwardly, because he knew whatever news was coming, it wouldn't be about to make his life easier.

Posie had flung herself in the chair opposite his own, sending a cascade of his important photographs of the Bond Street scene-of-crime spilling onto the floor. She had jabbed at an inside page of *The Times*.

'Richard, darling, it's just the perfectly oddest thing. Look at this.'

She slid the newspaper across the desk to him and he took it half-heartedly, like a man being handed a poisoned chalice. The front page showed the news of that day's General Election results: the landslide re-election of the conservative Stanley Baldwin as Prime Minister. There was a large photograph of Baldwin without a hat on, looking dishevelled somehow, despite wearing obviously expensive clothes, an eyebrow raised – as if in surprise at his good fortune – with his pipe clamped in the side of his mouth, in his trademark style.

'No, no, darling. The next page.'

Page two was busier, the stories cramped together. Most of the space seemed to be given up to Italian news, with stories of riots and anti-fascist protests taking place in Rome against Benito Mussolini's government. Posie reached over the desk impatiently and jabbed right down at the bottom, on the far right: a tiny thumb-nail box which almost vanished in the crease of the paper's centrefold.

'There. See?'

'Blink and you'd miss it, darling.' But he had frowned as he read the tiny news-report, tugging his fingers backwards through his thick hair as he did so.

Posie sat waiting, all a-jitter on the edge of her chair.

The story was short.

GIRL FALLS OFF CLIFF: ST MARGARET'S BAY, KENT

THE INQUEST WILL BE HEARD AT DOVER TOWN HALL TOMORROW (WED. 5TH NOVEMBER, 12 NOON) INTO THE TRAGIC DEATH OF MISS ELSIE MONCRIEFF, OF WHITE SHAW, ST MARGARET'S BAY. HER BODY WAS DISCOVERED VERY EARLY YESTERDAY MORNING (MONDAY 3RD NOVEMBER) BY A DOG WALKER.

MISS MONCRIEFF, HOUSEKEEPER TO THE FAMOUS FASHION DESIGN DUO, DOUGLAS & STONE, DIED ON SUNDAY NIGHT, 2nd NOVEMBER, IN INEXPLICABLE CIRCUMSTANCES. IT IS CURRENTLY BELIEVED THAT MISS MONCRIEFF ACCIDENTALLY FELL

OFF THE TREACHEROUS CLIFF KNOWN AS NESS POINT DURING A BAD STORM LATE AT NIGHT, BUT THE CORONER HAS (UNUSUALLY) RECORDED AN OPEN VERDICT.

IT SEEMS THERE MAY BE MORE TO THIS ACCIDENT AT THE CHIC RIVIERA RESORT OF ST MARGARET'S BAY THAN MEETS THE EYE. WE WILL BE REPORTING ON ANY DEVELOPMENTS.

Lovelace had looked up and raised an eyebrow. In truth he had had simply no idea why Posie should find this news so fascinating.

'Mnnn? What about it?' He was suddenly distracted by his pile of fallen photographs and also by his two secretaries who were gossiping too close outside his open door; friendly voices talking about stupid things. He needed to crack on.

'What is it, darling? Is it the Fashion House connection? That married couple who are never out of the press? Douglas & Stone? Don't tell me you know them? A slippery pair; something to do with the Prince of Wales, aren't they? Very unsuitable pals for him. They hardly seem *your* usual calibre of celebrity friends and acquaintances, I must say…'

Posie had huffed and puffed. She had got up and closed the door sharply.

'No, I don't know them and I've never met them. I don't go around collecting celebrity friends, by the way. My interest here is nothing to do with *them*. But don't you remember? I *told* you a few months back that I had received a very odd letter from a woman at St Margaret's Bay, in Kent. It was very late July, I think. I mentioned it specifically to you as we had worked on a case down there together some years back, remember?'

Lovelace frowned. 'Maypole Manor? That great house on top of the cliffs?'

'That's right. Although Maypole Manor has been bought and sold and bought and sold again since we were there three years ago. It's now unoccupied and I think there are plans afoot to demolish it entirely.'

Lovelace shrugged, unbothered. 'Good. Wretched place! But what's the connection to this newspaper story?'

Posie indicated towards *The Times* again. 'The funny thing is that it was *this* Elsie Moncrieff who wrote the strange letter to me. This poor dead woman, who has now fallen off a cliff.'

Lovelace hadn't been impressed. 'Well, it's a horrible way to die, my love, but these things *do* happen. What did the Moncrieff woman want of you, anyhow? What did her letter say?'

Posie bit at a burgundy fingernail. 'I'm going to go to the Grape Street Bureau and dig it out from the office filing now. I was just sitting waiting for my tea and crumpets to arrive at Lyons Cornerhouse on Trafalgar Square when I happened to chance upon this story. If I remember rightly, Elsie was very vague in the letter. She suggested there was something wrong at the place where she worked. *This* place, White Shaw, I presume...' Posie had wrinkled her brow, trying to recall the facts: she hated not having the information to hand.

'She never mentioned her famous employers, I'm sure of it. Miss Moncrieff wanted me to go down there and she would explain everything.'

Lovelace raised an eyebrow and kept it raised. 'Darling, have you considered that this poor woman was simply barmy? Maybe she took a voluntary running jump off that cliff on Sunday night? *That's* what was "wrong".'

'Suicide?'

Lovelace had shrugged. 'Well, perhaps she was off her head on something strong, eh? If she was exposed to the lifestyle of her employers, she'd have found it dashed easy to get her hands on any number of drugs; *if* the press are to be believed. Don't that couple have famously raucous parties at that beachside place of theirs?'

He picked up his Bond Street photographs carefully, stacking them together neatly, one by one. He checked his watch pointedly. Although he adored his future wife beyond all reasonable measure, he had a presentation to make within the hour.

He tried to wrap things up: 'Well, you didn't take Miss Moncrieff's case anyway, did you, my love? So you must have felt it was all fairly insignificant at the time.'

But Posie had shaken her head. 'I didn't take the case at the time as it didn't fit in with my travel plans. Elsie wrote to me at the end of July and I went to Italy for the whole of August – to San Gimignano – do you recall?'

Oh, yes. Richard Lovelace recalled.

It had been the longest month he'd ever got through, desperate for his new fiancée to come home. Desperate to know she hadn't changed her mind about him while out holidaying under the Tuscan sun.

Posie bit at her lip, defensive now. 'I wrote back to Elsie Moncrieff apologising that I couldn't come straight away, and I offered my services upon my return, in September; *if* that suited her. I was surprised not to receive a reply, but assumed things had all turned out for the best. But then a couple of days ago I found a pile of unsent, stamped mail – letters from *me* to my clients – all sitting stacked in Prudence's bottom drawer. She'd quite forgotten to post the wretched things. I had been looking for something else, something trivial – a packet of chocolate probably – and I came across the unsent letters quite by chance. Well, the awful thing is, my original reply to Elsie Moncrieff was among all the others; unsent, unread. So Elsie Moncrieff never knew that I did write back. That I wanted to help her…'

Lovelace had looked horrified. He hated sloppiness of any kind. It sent cold shivers down his spine. 'That's terrible! What on earth was Prudence's excuse?'

Posie half-grinned. 'Prudence has had her head in the clouds since this summer – ever since *your* Sergeant Rainbird jolly well went and proposed to her! I can only guess she forgot about them in a mad frenzy of wedding dress shopping.' She sighed. 'I was hopping mad, actually. I had it out with Prudence. Stern words. But now I've calmed down. What does it help if I'm angry at her? Most of the time she's a first-rate secretary and they're dashed difficult to find.'

And then Posie had rushed on, all the while wrapping herself back up in her expensive maroon woollen coat and matching beret, gathering up her newspaper and her beloved carpet bag. 'So, my love, you know me. I feel pretty awful about this whole thing. *Guilty*, somehow. As if I could have helped this poor woman in July, and I didn't.'

Posie had loitered at the door, Lovelace now rather frantically checking through some notes he had made for the speech he was about to give.

'I thought I'd just pop down to the Inquest, Richard darling.'

'Hmmm?'

'It's probably nothing, but I'd like to check it out. Satisfy myself everything was quite in order.'

'Hmmm.'

'It's *tomorrow*, Richard. So I'll be getting the early train from Victoria and heading on down to Dover. Are you listening to me? Actually, I'll stay in St Margaret's Bay, near where it all happened, at that very nice hotel, The Bay. I've already telephoned, and they were very happy to offer me a room, a suite actually, for a week or so.'

Lovelace suddenly snapped himself together. He had eyed Posie keenly, watchfully. He needed to be careful in his response, in his handling of her. Their marriage was supposed to be in six weeks' time. That meant there was still six weeks during which he could lose her. And they still hadn't agreed on a church. Or a venue. Nothing was booked, and no invitations sent, much to his chagrin.

This coltish girl.

'I see,' he said evenly. 'So you'll be away about a week, will you?'

'More or less. Not sure yet.'

'What about the fireworks and the bonfire on Clapham Common tomorrow night? It's Guy Fawkes Night. Phyllis will miss you terribly. And what about the wedding on Saturday? Surely you'll still come with me?'

It was Prudence, Posie's secretary's, wedding at the weekend. The long-awaited and mooned-over nuptials with Sergeant Rainbird.

Posie looked horrified. She'd forgotten. 'Oh, my golly! Of course, I'll attend with you. If needs be I can always come up specially for it and then hop on a train back down to Kent again afterwards, can't I? And I'm jolly sorry about the fireworks tomorrow with darling Phyllis. But it can't be helped I'm afraid.'

'And the appointment with the men to clear the flat tomorrow morning?'

'Oh!' She had shaken her head maddeningly. 'Oh my gosh! It had quite slipped my mind. But I absolutely must go to the Inquest. Is that all right, Richard? You look a bit glum. Can we simply cancel the men? Or can *you* attend and let them in? I *have* to go. You do understand, don't you?'

'It's fine, sweetheart. Of course, I understand.'

But if truth be told, it had seemed like the paper-thinnest of excuses for Posie to be upping sticks and rushing off to the South Coast like this.

No: he didn't understand. But Richard Lovelace loved Posie Parker and he'd get on with things as best he could.

Which was how he had found himself supervising

everything this morning, running out of time and humour.

Coming to his senses, he dashed to the window of Museum Chambers, pulled up the sash and hollered down into the street for his new man, Sergeant Fox, to come up to the flat as quickly as possible. The team of removal men were still carrying Alaric's things out at a snail's pace. The Decorator had also now finished his tea and was standing by, impatiently awaiting instructions, whistling in an intensely irritating way.

Once Sergeant Fox was inside Posie's flat, Lovelace was quick at dealing with things. He smartened himself up in just a few seconds, rolled down his shirtsleeves, patted down his unruly hair, all in the reflection of the glass frame of one of the hieroglyphs in Posie's lounge.

'Fox? You're going to stay here as long as it takes. I don't trust these removal fellas not to run away with the goods they're transporting. Supervise it all and do it efficiently. Oh, and get this chap to paint the room over there in pink. Several coats of the stuff. You hear me? I want a nice job done.'

'Pink, sir? Are you quite sure?'

'Absolutely.' The Inspector indicated the tins on the floor. '*You* take your pick of the colours, eh? Something relatively easy on the eye. If it's your choice then I can blame you when Posie hates it. Only joking!'

He passed across Posie's set of keys. 'You lock up when everyone's finished in here, won't you? I'm off. See how it feels to be a Sergeant? How well I'm using you now, Fox?'

'Sir?'

'I'm referring to your Sergeant's exams, lad. You did so well in passing them that I'm giving you all the best, most complicated jobs. Like choosing paint, and then watching it dry.'

'Very good, sir.'

Lovelace made to leave, wondering for the hundredth time how Posie was getting on right now, what she would find out at the Inquest, and what on earth she was really up to.

All the way back to his office he tried to tamp down his worry.

What was it about St Margaret's Bay which made him feel dreadfully on edge? In his mind's eye something dark and unpalatable seemed to rise up before him; the dregs of a memory, half-suppressed, half-forgotten. But what?

He remembered back to when Posie and he had worked the case at Maypole Manor. He had been happily, if staidly married back then, of course. Before the fire which had snatched his first wife, Molly, away from him forever. And Posie…well, she had had Alaric, who had been dashing around being dashing as usual.

Different times.

But the dead couldn't harm them now.

And the precise form of danger which had led them to St Margaret's Bay in the first place had been well and truly eradicated. So what uncertainty was clouding his mind? Whatever it was, he couldn't shake it from his thoughts during the entire drive back to Scotland Yard.

Good job then that he had taken measures; precautions as only he could.

Immediately after Posie had left his office yesterday he had made a telephone call to his previous Sergeant, Rainbird. Trusty, if unimaginative: a plodder who looked set to stay within the 'Sergeant' ranks for the rest of his life, but a reassuring policeman all the same.

Remembering the conversation gave Lovelace comfort now. He'd pulled rank. But he'd been acting on the orders of his heart – unusually – rather than his head.

'Rainbird?'

'Chief Commissioner?'

'The usual old "sir" will suffice. Just like before.'

'Sir?'

'Are you busy tomorrow, Rainbird?'

'I have leave booked, sir. I'll be taking a few days to prepare for my wedding this coming weekend.'

'All leave is cancelled. I need you to work tomorrow.'

'Oh?' The flatness in Rainbird's voice was not easily disguised.

'I need you on a train to Dover, to attend a Coroner's Inquest starting at noon. I'll send you the details.'

'I see, sir. Why is the Yard getting involved, sir? Something big, is it?'

'It could be. I don't yet know. Something or nothing, I suppose. You have my full authority to act as you see fit, Rainbird. A *carte blanche*, if you like. I need you to be my eyes and ears down there. Okay?'

'Oh, I see, sir.' Rainbird sounded hopeful all of a sudden. Scenting a sniff in the direction of promotion after having failed his Inspector's exams now twice in a row.

'Is there anything in particular I should be watching out for, sir?'

Lovelace had paused, and then coughed slightly apologetically. 'You can keep an eye out for my fiancée, Rainbird. But without making her suspicious, if you see what I mean.'

'You want me to follow Miss Parker, sir?'

'Not quite. No. That's too much. Just keep a friendly eye on the gal.'

There had been a slight pause. 'Do you believe her to be in danger, sir?'

'In truth I don't know, Sergeant. But I think that's what I am fearful of, yes.'

'Very good, sir.'

It wasn't good, but it was something, and this, Lovelace now thought to himself as his police driver swung through the iron gates of Scotland Yard, on the way to his meeting, was the best he could do in the circumstances.

* * * *

If you enjoyed this taster, you can download
the complete ebook or buy the paperback here:
https://www.amazon.com/dp/0992925495/

Historical Note

All of the characters in this book are fictional, unless specifically mentioned below. However, timings, general political events, and places (and descriptions of places) are historically accurate to the best of my knowledge, save for the exceptions listed below.

As in the other Posie Parker books, I refer to the First World War of 1914–1918 as the 'Great War' throughout, which is simpler for the modern reader, although it would not have been referred to in this way in 1924.

As ever, both Posie's work address in London (Grape Street, Bloomsbury, WC1) and her home address around the corner (Museum Chambers, WC1) are both very real, although you might have to do a bit of imagining to find her there.

1. (Throughout) The Swiss Church in London can be found (79, Endell Street, London WC2H 9DY) in Bloomsbury, exactly like in this story. Please note that the description of the Swiss Church in this story is much more akin to how the church appears today, rather than how it would have appeared in 1924.

   I am grateful to the Vicar of the Swiss Church, the Reverend Carla Maurer, for making time to show me around the church in summer 2019 and for answering my questions. I am also grateful to Mr Philip Maillardet, the Archivist at the Swiss Church, for his generous help in answering my questions about the church in 1924 and for his time in describing how the exits and entrances to the church would have worked.

2. Please note, I have described snow as falling on 6th December 1924. This is a fabrication of my own, as the weather conditions in London in that month were unusual, actually pretty mild and rainy, only falling to zero degrees at night, with no snow by day.

3. The Reverend René Hoffman de Visme (I call him Father Hoffman here for ease) was indeed the long-serving Vicar of the Swiss Church at this time, and his dates at the church are 1909–1937. I have used artistic licence with regard to his appearance and personality.

4. The Montague on the Gardens, where Posie and Richard have their Wedding Breakfast is at 15, Montague Street, London WC1B 5BJ, right next to the British Museum in Bloomsbury. Although it would not have existed in 1924 in its exact current incarnation, it would certainly have been a hotel. https://www.montaguehotel.com

5. Kettner's in Soho, the scene of Richard Lovelace's fake stag night, is a London institution; a restaurant and champagne bar which was set up in 1867 and has been forever associated with creative types. Oscar Wilde and Agatha Christie were frequent visitors.

https://www.kettners.com

6. New Scotland Yard in 1924 was where I have described it to be, and those exact buildings are now known

as the Norman Shaw Buildings. Westminster Pier (on Victoria Embankment) is indeed directly below the former Scotland Yard buildings, but the tunnel connecting them is a fiction of my own. The present-day New Scotland Yard is located right next door to its 1924 incarnation.

* * * *

Thank you for joining Posie Parker and her friends.

Enjoyed *Marriage is Murder?* (A Posie Parker Mystery #9)? Here's what you can do next.

If you loved this book and have a tiny moment to spare, I would really appreciate a short review on the page where you bought the book. Your help in spreading the word about the series is invaluable and really appreciated, and reviews make a big difference to helping new readers find the series.

Posie's other cases are available in e-book and paperback formats from Amazon, as well as in selected bookstores.

They are also available in audiobook format from Audible and many other audiobook retailers.

You can find all of the other books, available for purchase, listed here in chronological order:

http://www.amazon.com/L.B.-Hathaway/e/
B00LDXGKE8

and

http://www.amazon.co.uk/L.B.-Hathaway/e/
B00LDXGKE8

You can sign up to be notified of new releases, pre-release specials, free short stories and the chance to win Amazon gift-vouchers here:

http://www.lbhathaway.com/contact/newsletter/

About the Author

Cambridge-educated, British-born L.B. Hathaway writes historical fiction. She worked as a lawyer at Lincoln's Inn in London for almost a decade before becoming a full-time writer. She is a lifelong fan of detective novels set in the Golden Age of Crime, and is an ardent Agatha Christie devotee.

Her other interests, in no particular order, are: very fast downhill skiing, theatre-going, drinking strong tea, Tudor history, exploring castles and generally trying to cram as much into life as possible. She lives in Switzerland with her husband and young family.

The Posie Parker series of cosy crime novels span the 1920s. They each combine a core central mystery, an exploration of the reckless glamour of the age and a feisty protagonist who you would love to have as your best friend.

To find out more and for news of new releases and giveaways, go to:
http://www.lbhathaway.com

Connect with L.B. Hathaway online:
(e) author@lbhathaway.com
(t) @LbHathaway
(f) https://www.facebook.com/
pages/L-B-Hathaway-books/1423516601228019
(Goodreads) http://www.goodreads.com/author/
show/8339051.L_B_Hathaway

Made in the USA
Coppell, TX
17 July 2020

31149137R00067